D0276990

STRIKING
OUT

STRIKING OUT

IAN WRIGHT &
MUSA OKWONGA

■SCHOLASTIC

For my brother, Maurice Albert Wright.

Ian Wright

For Richard Diffenthal, Ian Toothill and Graham Joyce.

Musa Okwonga

Published in the UK by Scholastic, 2021
Euston House, 24 Eversholt Street, London, NW1 1DB

Scholastic Ireland, 89E Lagan Road, Dublin Industrial Estate,
Glasnevin, Dublin, D11 HP5F

SCHOLASTIC and associated logos are trademarks and/or
registered trademarks of Scholastic Inc.

Text © Ian Wright and Musa Okwonga, 2021

Illustrations © Benjamin Wachenje, 2021

The right of Ian Wright, Musa Okwonga and Benjamin Wachenje
to be identified as the authors and illustrator of this work has been
asserted by them under the Copyright, Designs and Patents Act 1988.

ISBN 978 07023 0686 0

A CIP catalogue record for this book is available from the British Library.

Printed by CPI Group (UK) Ltd, Croydon, CR0 4YY

Paper made from wood grown in sustainable forests and other controlled sources.

1 3 5 7 9 10 8 6 4 2

www.scholastic.co.uk

PART 1

LOOKING FOR YOU

THE FEAR

One spring evening, as Jerome walked back to his flat, he thought what he so often did: *this doesn't feel like my home. It's just a place I have to stay until the day I can move out.* But he was only thirteen, and it was going to be five years before he could do that. For now, he had to stay where he was, with his mum, who he loved so much, and with her boyfriend, Larry, who he did not.

As Jerome walked, the darkness started to roll over his shoulders, broken only by the soft orange glow of the street lights. He looked down, his shadow reaching in front of him, and he imagined that these were not street lights but floodlights, and that the cracked tarmac beneath his feet was the smooth grass of a football stadium.

In his mind, the stadium was full: it was a Premier League game, on a Monday evening. *'That's the exciting* new teenager Jerome Jackson,' said the TV commentator, 'playing up front as the lone striker. Here's an interesting story about Jackson — he was offered the number nine shirt by his club, but he refused, because he wants to wear the number fifteen instead. He says that he wants to make it famous. What a confident young man he is! Let's see what he can do against Everton tonight.'

For just a moment, he was Jerome Jackson, the brilliant new centre forward for Millwall, but then his daydream disappeared, and he was just Jerome again, shuffling back to his road. He knew if he got there too early then it would just be him and Larry, the way it often was on weeknights. He would have to wait a couple of hours for his mum, and when she did return from work, just before nine, she was always exhausted. She would come all the way from her job in Harrow, where she worked as a caterer. Every now and then Jerome would wait for her on the platform at Hackney Central station, just a fifteen-minute walk from their flat, to escort her home. A little bit of the tiredness would fall away from her face as soon as she saw him. But Jerome hadn't met her at the station in a while.

Jerome came off the main road and into his estate. He looked up from the corner of the courtyard, towards the first floor of his building, and grimaced as he saw that the light was on in his kitchen. *Oh, no,* thought Jerome. *Larry is in our place. I thought he was still going to be at the pub with his friends.* And that's when it started. That's when it came for him: the fear.

Whenever Larry was around unexpectedly, Jerome got the fear in every part of his body. First there was a tumbling in his gut, like he was going to be sick, and he pressed his hand against a nearby wall to stop himself falling over. Then his vision blurred, the way it did when he had a bad headache. And, for just a second, he couldn't breathe.

Jerome felt this way about Larry because he knew that Larry didn't really want him in the flat. Like he was just someone who was in the way, who stopped Larry spending more time with his mum. Jerome never told his mum exactly how he felt about Larry, about the fear. He didn't want her to worry. He knew that if he just stayed strong, he would be OK. He leaned against the wall a little longer, then he slowly breathed in, out, in, out. *That's better*, he thought.

He dragged his feet up the steps, then stood outside his front door and took a few short breaths, preparing himself for the contest. There was always a contest. It seemed that each time he saw Jerome, Larry would try to challenge him, try to make him feel uncomfortable or unhappy about something. As Jerome raised his key to his front door, he wondered what Larry had in store this time.

Jerome turned the key and heard Larry's voice rumble down the hallway.

'Steph? Steph, is that you?'

'No,' said Jerome, 'it's me.'

Somewhere in the darkness, Larry grunted. Jerome stepped into the flat, and the next thing he felt was pain.

'Ow!'

Jerome turned on the hallway light. Looking down, he saw that he had stepped on one of Larry's boots, which were lying in his path. The sting dragged its way across his left ankle like a piece of barbed wire. He clamped his hands around his ankle, trying to stop the hurt from spreading. It worked, a little, and after a few seconds he gingerly stood upright again.

His bedroom was to his left, and he wanted to go straight in there and put on some music, but he knew it was best not to ignore Larry. If he did that, Larry would only complain to his mum later. He would tell her: *that boy Jerome has got bad manners; you're not raising him right.* So he walked past the kitchen and then to his right, towards the living room and the chatter of the television.

As Jerome walked in, Larry didn't look up. He was on the sofa on the opposite side of the room, spread all across it like a bedsheet across a washing line. He looked exhausted. His head sagged to one side, as if it was almost too heavy to stay on his neck, and his left arm rested on the windowsill, up against the curtains. *How long he is,* Jerome thought. Larry's left foot was dangled over one arm of the sofa, his toes pointing at the television. His right foot was planted in the middle of the living-room floor, an anchor covered in a thick white sock. Next to his right foot was a plate, scraped clean of everything except four bones and a few grains of brown rice.

'Your mum's chicken was good,' said Larry.

I bet it was amazing, thought Jerome sadly. *But I need to be careful what I say.* Talking to Larry was like holding a match near a firework. Anything you said could make him go off.

'I hope your work was OK today,' said Jerome.

'Hard,' said Larry, 'not that you'd know anything about that.' Larry worked as a removals man, and so he spent most of his week carrying heavy boxes up and down stairs. His dark green tracksuit bottoms were scuffed with dust, and his black T-shirt tugged at his pale skin as his chest rose and fell.

'Where were you working today?'

Larry looked up, suspicious. Why was Jerome being so nice?

'Down in Rochester,' he said carefully.

'Oh,' said Jerome, 'that's a lot of travel. At least two hours there and back?'

'Three,' groaned Larry, sounding more relaxed. 'And then we had to clear out this rich bloke's flat and move him back into Bromley. The mess in there, you wouldn't believe.'

Jerome nodded in sympathy. 'Can I get you some tea?' he asked.

'Yes you can,' said Larry.

'Your usual? Milk, two sugars?' asked Jerome.

'Yes, that's it,' said Larry. 'Don't show off.' Jerome scooped up Larry's plate from the floor and walked round the corner into the kitchen. When he turned on the light, he sighed with disappointment.

His hungry eyes went to the cooker, where there were two small metal pots. One of them carried nothing more than a wooden spoon and a single red kidney bean. The other one, thankfully, contained one remaining chicken leg, which Jerome seized at once and ran under his nose, smelling its sweet spices before tearing away the meat with his teeth. *Mum's cooking is just amazing*, he thought. He looked round the door frame and back towards the living room. *I just wish Larry could have left me a bit more.*

He washed up Larry's plate, dried it and put it away in the cupboard. Then he boiled the water, and the growl in the plastic kettle was the same as the growl in his own stomach. He poured the water into Larry's favourite mug, the dark blue one with the green inside, and he let the tea brew for as long as it took him to calm down. He tried to remember what his mum always told him about being a good Christian, that if someone slaps you on one cheek, you should turn the other one for them to slap. *But what if they keep slapping you on both cheeks?* he thought.

He took Larry's tea back into the living room, and sat down in a nearby armchair, watching as he tasted it.

'Hmmm. You're getting good at this,' said Larry. 'You didn't get one for yourself?'

'No, I'm fine,' said Jerome.

Larry flicked through the different channels – quiz show, reality TV, news, then back to quiz show. A man was being cheered on by a crowd as he tried to win a large amount of money. The man answered a question incorrectly and the crowd groaned.

'Absolute loser,' said Larry. He flicked through again and found a car chase through a busy city. He nodded, and his head sagged back against his neck. Finally at ease, Jerome started to drift asleep too.

'Just look at you two! Like a couple of sleepy bears.'

Jerome heard a woman's voice: so gentle, like a dentist telling a young patient not to be afraid. His eyes flew open. *Mum!*

She was standing in the doorway, her hair rising up above her headband in a soft, frazzled bun, her cheeks pushing out a smile, her arms clutching a large white cardboard box. Jerome leapt up from his armchair, offering it to her, but she shook her head.

'No,' she said, 'today, the special treatment is for you.' She stopped, and her smile was suddenly less tired. 'Many happy returns, birthday boy!'

Now it was the turn of Larry's eyes to fly open.

'What – what?' gasped Larry, as Jerome's mum flipped open the box to reveal Jerome's favourite cake – chocolate sponge with vanilla buttercream icing. For a moment Jerome was in heaven as he imagined how each slice would taste as it melted on his tongue. But then he remembered who he was living with, and he felt sick again.

'Jerome, it's your birthday?' spluttered Larry.

Oh no, thought Jerome. 'Yes,' he said. 'I'm thirteen today.'

'Why on earth didn't you say anything?' Larry was now sitting upright, his body as tight as a tennis net.

'Didn't think you'd care,' said Jerome, but he said it so quickly and quietly that it was only a mumble, and no one heard it.

'Larry!' said Jerome's mum, sounding shocked. 'I reminded you of this just last night!' She closed the box. 'I told you – when Jerome gets home, share the food I cooked, and then we will have some cake tonight!' She frowned. 'You did share the food, didn't you?'

'Of course I did, Steph!' Larry glanced at Jerome, and the look on his face was a mix of fear and anger. *Don't you dare tell her*, it said.

'Yes, he did,' said Jerome. 'We were so tired from eating the chicken that we fell asleep.'

Larry nodded. 'That's right.'

'Hmm,' said Stephanie. She wasn't convinced. But she was too worn out from work and from carrying that heavy cake all the way home to argue.

'Mum,' said Jerome, 'please, sit down. Tell you what – why don't we all have some cake now. You two just relax and I'll sort everything out.' He took the cake into the kitchen and cut slices for each of them, serving them on to his mum's best crockery: the white saucers with the floral print. He placed the saucers on to a tray and walked back into the living room. Larry and Stephanie were sitting there in silence. On the television, which was now on mute, two men fought over a gun.

'Jerome, I'm so sorry,' said Stephanie. 'It was such a busy day, and I knew I would get home late. I wanted to do something nicer than this for you—'

'Me too,' said Larry desperately.

Jerome calmly put the tray down on the living-room table.

'It's OK,' he said. 'Everyone was too busy. Thanks so much for the cake, Mum. It looks amazing. I think I'll have mine in my room.'

'Jerome, don't,' said Stephanie. 'We should eat it as a family.'

Walk away now, thought Jerome. *Don't make her say please.*

'Mum, it's OK,' said Jerome.

'Look what you've done by forgetting, Larry! You've upset him!'

'Leave it out, Stephanie. He's playing you!'

Jerome took his saucer to his bedroom and locked his door, and a few minutes later the shouting really started.

Jerome pulled off his trainers, lay on his bed and put on his headphones.

He didn't want to hear Larry arguing with his mum.

But he also didn't want to listen to himself thinking: *Jerome, that was so selfish of you; all you had to do was eat some cake with your mum and Larry, but no, you had to go and start an argument and then leave.*

Jerome turned the volume up to drown out the thoughts. 'Today I'm thirteen,' he said to himself quietly. 'I can move out when I'm eighteen. Just five more years, Jerome. Just five more years.'

2

SUDDENLY FREE

No matter how sad Jerome was, he always looked forward to playing football. He played whenever he could: before school or on Saturday mornings, before he unloaded groceries for pocket money on Saturday afternoons, at lunchtimes or just before the sun went down, or best of all on Sundays for his local team. Jerome knew that if he just went outside with a ball and put his head down and ran fast enough then he could escape all the sadness. There were so many times when he would jog down the steps of his building, roll a football out in front of him, and nudge it forward with his left or right foot, sprinting after it over the tarmac of the car park. He would pretend that each parked car was a huge defender coming to tackle him. Just before he got to each car, he would flick the ball over its bumper with the edge of his toes and then rush round to collect it on the other side, sometimes before it touched the ground. 'Jerome,' someone would usually shout out from the building above, 'don't you touch my car!' But Jerome never did.

As he came out of his estate and on to the busy main road, Jerome would dribble the ball up on to the pavement and then along its edge, as if he were walking along a tightrope. Cars rushed past on one side of him, and pedestrians strode by him on the other, telling him to stop doing something so dangerous, but Jerome didn't notice them. All he saw was that ten-centimetre-wide strip of concrete ahead of him and that football, spinning slowly and delicately under his control.

No one knew why Jerome was brilliant at this game. Both his parents had been good athletes – his dad had liked running, and his mum had been on her school team, doing long jump – but no one, not his aunts or his uncles, had been much good at kicking a ball. It was a mystery to everyone but Reverend Benjamin, who taught Bible classes every Sunday at the local Methodist church. 'Maybe,' said Reverend Benjamin, 'someone just gave Jerome a very special gift.'

Reverend Benjamin was the first person who had realized just how good Jerome was at football. There was a small lawn at the back of the church building, where you weren't really supposed to walk unless you were taking photos for somebody's wedding. When nobody was looking, Reverend Benjamin would sneak out and kick a ball around on there before the service. One day, he had kicked the ball too hard, and it went behind a fence. He was just on his way to fetch the ball when it came flying back, past his face, so fast that he had to duck before it broke his nose. Looking up, he saw Martin, Jerome's father, coming round the corner. Reverend Benjamin was about to shout at him, but then Martin said, 'No, that wasn't me – that wasn't me who kicked the ball at you. That was my son.' And then the two men looked down at this grinning three-year-old boy in a black suit and brand-new shiny black shoes, who could already hit the ball as hard as someone three times his age. They were quiet for a while, and then Reverend Benjamin spoke. 'It looks like your boy is special,' he said.

'Oh,' said Martin, smiling and running his hand through Jerome's hair, 'I knew Jerome was special. I just didn't know he was special at football too.'

As Jerome dribbled the ball along the pavement, he remembered his dad, and then he lowered his head and jogged a little quicker, because he didn't want the people in the street to see the tears forming in his eyes. When Jerome's dad was alive, it had felt like the world was sunny all the time – but three years ago he had died, and it felt like it had been raining in Jerome's life ever since.

Everyone who met Jerome's dad had loved him. 'Martin was such a good man. He was here first thing every Sunday, setting up the chairs,' they would tell Jerome at church. 'He would always carry my shopping upstairs,' said Mrs Malone, the old lady who lived two floors above them. 'He painted my new kitchen for free, and he didn't even ask for anything,' said Benedict, the man on the ground floor who got sick when he was thirty and couldn't work any more. That was Martin Jackson. He was always helping other people; he was always fixing other people's lives, but when he needed help the doctors couldn't fix him.

Martin and Jerome had looked just like each other. They had bushy, curly black hair which would grow two inches tall if you didn't cut it for just a few weeks, and Martin used to comb Jerome's hair out just the same as his. When Stephanie saw them each morning, she would shake her head but she couldn't stop smiling. 'Look at you,' she would say. 'My boys.' They went everywhere together: they weren't just dad and son; they were a team. One day Mrs Malone called them Big Tin and Little Tin, because she said that Jerome was just a smaller copy of Martin, and she never stopped calling Jerome that, even after Big Tin died.

Jerome would dribble his ball down nearly every street in his area of Hackney, but the only place he avoided was down the street where his dad was buried. Whenever he came close to it, he swerved away to the right, as if it was the one defender on the football pitch who he didn't want to go near. He couldn't look at his dad's grave, that small white stone sticking out of the edge of the grass like a lonely tooth. His mum went to visit it every month and when she got back Jerome would always ask, 'How was Dad?' And his mum would say, 'He is well, he misses you. He asks when you are going to see him.' But Jerome didn't go, not once.

He still couldn't believe his dad was gone. The day Dad died had just been so normal. He had gone to decorate a big house in West London and he said he would be back late because it was such a long job. But he didn't come back that night. The next morning there was a knock on the door and when Jerome's mum opened it there was a policeman with a very serious look on his face. 'Please can I come in?' the policeman had asked. 'It's about your husband, Martin.' They had found Martin lying a few metres from the Underground station, where he was running to catch one of the last trains back home. They had taken him to the hospital and the doctor had said that Martin's heart had just stopped. 'Like a clock?' asked Jerome. 'Yes, like a clock,' said the policeman. 'So you can't just start it up again?' asked Jerome. 'The doctors tried so hard,' said the policeman. 'But there are some clocks you just can't start again. The pieces inside them are too broken.' And then the policeman went away.

Jerome didn't understand how his dad could be broken. All these old people in Jerome's building were still alive and when his dad had died, he'd still looked new. His mum couldn't explain it and that was the day she became broken too. She started sleeping so much that sometimes she wouldn't get up when her alarm went off, and Jerome would have to go into her room and wake her up so she wouldn't be late for work. She stopped watching her favourite programmes, the quiz shows that she and Jerome's dad would watch together, and she stopped singing to herself. The house became a lot quieter after that. A few months later, while she was still broken, she met Larry.

Jerome reached the end of the pavement and stopped at the traffic lights, gripping the ball softly with the sole of his right foot. He was still feeling sad, and so he needed to find somewhere he could run faster. This was a day when he didn't want to bump into anyone he knew. He just wanted to be alone with his thoughts, and so he needed to get off the main road.

As he waited for the green man to appear, he quickly looked around at the area where he had grown up. It had changed so much in the time he had been there. The sandwich shop and the bike shop and the corner store were all gone, and now there were just flats, flats, flats. The rich people lived there. One of the new apartment buildings even had an underground car park, and sometimes Jerome would stand near it and watch the residents arriving, their sleek expensive vehicles sliding down into the darkness like seals plunging into the sea. Sometimes Jerome wished he lived there too.

'You'll never live there,' laughed Aaron when Jerome told him. Aaron was one of Jerome's oldest friends who lived on the same estate. He was only fifteen minutes older than Jerome, but sometimes it felt like fifteen years, because he always had something clever to say. Aaron pulled up his sleeve and tapped a finger on his skin. 'Even if you become a big footballer,' he told Jerome, 'they'll never let people who look like us buy a flat in there.'

Jerome shook his head. 'I'll do it one day,' he said.

'If you do,' said Aaron, flexing one of his biceps, 'I'll move all of your stuff in for free. You just have to give me one bedroom in return.'

Jerome laughed. 'That doesn't sound like it's for free, Aaron.'

Aaron tapped his forehead slowly. 'You see, Jerome?' he said, pretending to be serious. 'I told you I would give you a good price.'

Jerome loved Aaron, but he didn't see him so much these days. Last week, he saw him near the cinema with two girls, and Aaron asked Jerome to join them. But Jerome had said no.

'I've got to practise finishing with my left foot,' said Jerome.

Aaron rolled his eyes. 'You said that last time.'

'I know but I need to get it right. I missed a good chance with it last week.'

'Practise all you like,' said Aaron, 'you're not going to get any better, playing at that level. Not for a local team like Hackney Stallions.'

'But I like it there.'

'That's because it's easy for you. When are you going

to make the step up? When are you going to try for the big clubs again?'

'I'll do it when I'm ready,' said Jerome. 'I'm just trying to get my confidence back.'

'You've been saying that for years,' said Aaron.

Jerome noticed one of the girls looking at him. Her eyes made his skin sizzle, like he was a piece of bacon on the grill. 'What's your friend's name?' she said.

'Jerome,' said Aaron. 'His name is Jerome.'

'I'm Michelle,' said the girl, 'and this is Amira.' Amira folded her arms and stared off down the road, totally uninterested.

'Jerome, we never hang out any more,' said Aaron.

'I know,' said Jerome. 'I'm sorry.'

'What's wrong, Jerome?' said Aaron. 'I text you, no replies for days. It's like you're hiding from me.'

'I'm not hiding,' said Jerome. Now he could feel both Michelle and Amira watching him. One pair of eyes was hot, the other pair was cold. 'It's just – it sometimes feels like this neighbourhood is a big football pitch, you know? There's the busy, loud parts of the pitch where all the action happens – the midfield, and the penalty area. And then there's the wings – the edges of the pitch, the quiet bits. It's like – you like the midfield and the penalty area. And I like the wings. And that's why I don't see you.'

'Oh my God, Jerome.' Aaron put his head in his hands. 'Not everything in life is football.'

'That's one of the weirdest things I've ever heard,' said

Amira. 'Come on, Aaron. The film is starting soon. They are already showing the trailers.'

'I don't think it's weird,' said Michelle. 'I think it's cute.'

Jerome could not look at her. He checked his skin to see if it was still sizzling. It was.

'I'll see you,' said Jerome.

'Answer your text messages,' said Aaron.

Jerome hadn't seen him since then, and he hadn't answered his texts. He looked up at the traffic lights, and the green man was standing there. Jerome crossed the road, turning left down a peaceful street. There were no flats here, just two rows of houses, watched over by an oak tree so tall and old that Jerome's mum called it Grandpa. This street was the quickest way to the local park, and Jerome came down here at least three times a week. When he was halfway down, he slowed to wave at one of the open windows on the ground floor of a house, and two small children ran to the glass to greet him. Tobi and Femi, the four-year-old twins, treated Jerome like a celebrity whenever they saw him. 'Mum,' shouted Tobi, while Femi waved back. 'It's Jerome, the footballer!'

'Yes, it's Jerome the footballer,' said Mrs Ayandele, as she joined them at the window. 'Not so loud, people are still sleeping.' She put a hand on each of her children's shoulders.

'Can you do your trick for us?' asked Femi.

Jerome nodded. He flicked the ball up with his left foot, gripping it between his left shoulder and his left cheek, and then he let it fall towards the ground, bringing it to a stop on top of his left foot. He turned to Tobi and Femi, and he bowed, as he always did, and they clapped and cheered, as they always did.

'Thank you very much, Jerome,' said Mrs Ayandele. 'How is your mother doing?'

She never asked him how Larry was doing.

'She's good,' said Jerome. 'Tired, but good.'

'Please send her my best wishes,' said Mrs Ayandele. 'God bless that woman. Come on you two,' she said to the twins. 'Your breakfast is getting cold.'

Jerome watched them retreat into their home, and then he nudged the ball forward over the pavement. He didn't feel so sad now – seeing the children had cheered him up. He came to the edge of the park, which was still empty. The top of the grass was silver with morning dew. Jerome rolled the ball on to the field and ran after it: fast, alone, and suddenly free.

3

ABSOLUTE WORLDY

It was Sunday morning, which meant that Jerome was sitting in a dressing room, getting ready for a football match. His team, Hackney Stallions, had a game in the second round of the East London Cup against Leyton Wanderers, who had beaten them two years ago. Jerome hadn't been in the team back then, but he had heard all about how good Leyton were. He had also heard how much they liked to talk.

'Jerome, you need to be careful today,' said Steve, his team's manager. 'This team is very loud, and very mean. They are going to say a lot of nasty things to try to distract you. You'll have to keep your focus.'

Jerome nodded, but he wasn't really listening to Steve. He was busy listening to everything else: to the sound of his teammates' studs clattering against the floor as they put their boots on, to the shouts of the boys in the corridor, and to his own heart, which was drumming with excitement against the insides of his ribs. He looked up at the blackboard, where Steve had drawn the diagram of how he wanted the team to play. Ofori in goal; Lannoy, Wreh, Okot and Fysass in defence; French, Todorovic, West, Weber, Liu in midfield; and up front all by himself, Jackson. Jerome, the lone striker.

Some people didn't like being the centre forward, because there was too much pressure to score goals. Jerome loved it. His favourite thing was when someone passed him the ball and he was running through towards the goal, and he could hear everyone go quiet as they saw him approaching the goalkeeper. They went quiet because they knew he was going to score, because that's what Jerome always did. He already had thirty-one goals in twenty-two games, and every time he put the ball in the net, he had the same celebration. He held his right fist in the air, opening and closing it three times, counting out the number fifteen with his fingers: five, five, five. When anyone asked him what he was doing, he just told them, fifteen is my lucky number, but he never explained why.

'Hey, Jerome,' called Manny, Hackney Stallions' captain. 'How many are you going to get for us today?'

'However many it takes to win,' said Jerome. 'We can't lose to these.'

Manny grinned. 'Right answer,' he said. 'When you lose to Leyton, they never let you forget it.'

Manny had seen two of the Leyton boys last week on the train, and when they recognized him, they had laughed at him. 'We are going to chain you Stallions up,' said one of them. The other one put his hands around his neck, as if he was choking. 'You Stallions play such pretty football,' the boy continued, 'but you're scared of winning.'

When Manny told Jerome this story, Jerome scowled, but he didn't say anything.

'Watch out, everyone,' said Victor, 'Jerome's got that look on his face.'

'What look?' asked Jerome. He looked up and most of the people in the dressing room had their eyes on him, including Steve.

'That cold, angry look. As if you are going to eat their defenders like fried rice.'

The only person who wasn't looking at Jerome was staring out of the dressing room window. Lucas, their goalkeeper, was standing on one of the benches and squinting at something far away. After a few seconds he turned around and announced to his teammates:

'I swear I just saw Ian Wright.'

Rob, Jason and Ade, three of the four Arsenal fans on the team, sprinted to the window, jumping alongside Lucas on the bench and trying to see for themselves. Liam, the fourth Arsenal fan, ran out into the corridor and down the hall without a word, the rattle of his studs fading into the distance.

'You might well have seen him,' said Steve. 'He's here now and then – I think he knows someone who plays in one of the other leagues.'

The rattle of the studs returned down the hall and Liam's face – his cheeks bright pink with excitement – appeared in the frame of the door.

'Yes,' he cried. 'It's definitely him!'

Now all of the boys began to run outside, nearly knocking Liam over as they did so.

'Guys, wait!' shouted Steve. 'Who's going to take the bag of footballs down to the pitch?' But Steve was too late: everyone was already gone, his team talk forgotten. He sighed, slung the bag over his shoulder, and followed his players out on to Hackney Marshes.

On some days, Hackney Marshes felt like the best place in London to play football: maybe the best place in the world. Today was one of those days. This area of land was a never-ending green field which stretched all the way to the horizon, and everywhere you looked, there was a game going on – nearly a hundred of them at the same time. Over in one corner, you could see a small rising cloud of white smoke: this came from a stall where the hungry players could go for lunch after their matches. If you were lucky, the wind would blow the smell of the delicious food your way, and then you would rush over to buy some too. A few teams had brought along stereos and speakers, so that they could play their favourite music during the games. If you listened carefully, you could hear which artists had new singles out that week.

This Sunday, there was more of a buzz than usual, because Ian Wright was there. He had come to see his friend's son play for Highbury Corner, and even though he wore a black hat, black sunglasses and black scarf, everyone recognized Ian at once. Most of the adults on Hackney Marshes that day, from the ones who ran the food stall to the parents who had come to support their children, had grown up watching Ian play football for Arsenal, Crystal Palace, West Ham, England and more. And so, when they saw him striding across the grass, they called out to him as if they were still teenagers.

'Oi, Wrighty! Give us a wave!' one of them called, as Ian walked past.

'I can do better than that,' he said, and gave the man a bow before walking on.

'Ian Wright, Wright, Wright!' chanted another parent, just as they had done when they sat in the crowd at Arsenal games. He nodded towards them and smiled.

'Hey, Wrighty! Can you sign this for me?' Ian stopped to sign a woman's football shirt, and soon a crowd formed around him, all waiting to talk to him about this goal they'd seen him score or about how he was their favourite player back in the day. By the time that Jerome and his teammates got outside, there were already a few dozen people waiting to speak to Ian.

'Oh no!' said Lucas. 'Look at all those people. We're never going to get to speak to him.'

'Yeah, it's going to take hours to get to the front!' cried Rob. 'And kick-off is in fifteen minutes.'

'It's not going to take *hours*,' said Jerome, shaking his head. Rob was always exaggerating. Last week he said that someone set a new world record – that they could run a hundred metres in seven seconds. The week before that, he said that a cow had twenty stomachs – that's how it could make so much milk.

'OK, it won't take hours,' admitted Rob. 'But we still don't have time.'

Disappointed, the boys jogged over to their pitch, which was in the very middle of the Marshes. That was where they got their second piece of bad news of the day.

'Oh my God,' said Rob, looking at the team that they were going to play. 'They are giants.'

They were not giants, but they were very big. Most of them were ten centimetres taller than Manny, who was the Stallions' tallest player.

'Look, here come the little Stallions,' mocked one of them, making their teammates laugh.

'That's one of the boys I saw on the train,' said Manny, his voice suddenly glum.

Jerome looked at the opposition before turning to Manny. 'Why didn't you tell us he was so big?'

'Because he was one of the smaller ones,' said Manny.

'Come on,' said Steve, calling his team to one side of the pitch. 'No need to be negative. They are a big team, we already knew that, and they have a lot of skill. But we've got plenty of tricks of our own.'

'We do,' said Victor. 'We've got Jerome.'

Jerome didn't respond. He looked across at the defenders that he would be playing against, watching them warm up before kick-off. Everyone else on his team saw large, confident boys, but Jerome saw something else. *These boys are too comfortable*, he thought. *Life is too easy for them. They are not desperate. Not like me.* As they laughed and passed a ball among themselves, Jerome felt the blood inside his chest start to fizz with anger. *They think they're going to walk right over us*, he thought. *Like we're a mat for their dirty, muddy boots.* Jerome turned back towards his teammates.

'When we walk past their dressing room at the end of the game,' he said, 'I don't want to hear anything. I want them to feel so sad they can't even speak. I don't want them to talk until they've got off the train home.'

'Whoa,' said Manny. 'Jerome, you're sounding kind of scary, bro.'

But Jerome had already walked away towards the centre circle. *I sound scary*, he thought. *Good.* And then the whistle blew, and the game began.

***

After the first half, the Hackney Stallions sat by the side of the pitch in shock. As Steve passed around a bowl of orange slices, they each took one and nodded their thanks, too exhausted to talk.

'The good news,' said Steve, 'is that we are only losing 2–0. The bad news,' he continued, 'is that we should be losing by seven. And if we carry on like this, we will be.' He pointed at Lucas, who was breathing as heavily as if he had just run ten miles. 'That man there,' he announced, 'is already the man of the match. I don't care what anyone does in the second half – Lucas, you are a hero. I think I counted six or seven brilliant saves. Well done, you. Great job.'

The rest of the team murmured their agreement. They knew Leyton would be good, but not this good. They had scored their first goal after thirty-seven seconds, a swirling free kick into the top corner. Then they had scored again eight minutes later, a penalty after a foul on their striker. The rest of the half had just been attack after attack, with the Stallions defending however they could. Leyton hit the post twice and the crossbar twice, and the only other thing that had stopped them was Lucas.

'Jerome, we need more from you this half,' said Steve.

'I'm ready,' said Jerome, 'but the ball hasn't come to me.'

'Then come back into our half and get it,' Steve

replied. 'Sometimes the ball won't get to you. You have to go looking for it.'

As Leyton Wanderers walked towards their positions for the start of the match, eyeballing the exhausted Stallions players and smirking to each other, Jerome stared at them one by one. Instead of each of their faces, he imagined Larry's face. Each of these boys was suddenly his mum's boyfriend: mean, snarling, trying to stop him from living the life he wanted. But, just like Larry, they wouldn't stop him. They couldn't.

'Let them talk now,' said Jerome. 'You'll see.'

That second half, it was Leyton's turn to be shocked. As soon as the game started again, Jerome was everywhere. First, he ran back to the edge of his own area, to help his defenders play the ball away from goal. Then he tackled Leyton's captain so hard that he cracked one of his shinpads. And then, two minutes later, came the moment that made everyone stop: when the ball dropped towards Jerome forty yards from goal. Just before it touched the ground, Jerome thrashed it with his left foot. The ball soared high into the air, as if it was going to fly clear over the crossbar, and then, as everyone watched, it plunged suddenly, falling as fast as a rock dropped from a cliff, and swerved just beneath the crossbar and into the net. The ball flew so fast that the goalkeeper didn't even move.

Jerome turned around to see all his teammates running towards him, screaming with joy. He only just had time to do his favourite celebration – raising his hand in the air and flashing his fingers three times – before they jumped on him, and he was suddenly under a pile of his friends. And then they heard a huge roar. Several teams, who had already finished playing their own matches, had been walking past the pitch when they saw Jerome shoot. When the ball went in, they all stopped and hollered.

'Did you see the dip on that?'

'Wish I'd recorded that on my phone. It would have gone viral!'

When Jerome finally finished celebrating, he stood up and looked to the side of the pitch, where he saw a man in a black hat and black sunglasses and a black scarf watching him with a smile as bright as the sun.

'Oh my days,' the man yelled. 'Best goal I've seen this year. Absolute worldy!'

'Jerome!' said Manny. 'Ian Wright is cheering for your goal!'

'Oh my God!' said Jerome.

'Excuse me,' said the referee, holding the match ball and pointing to the halfway line. 'Great goal, but we do have a match to play here.'

Jerome ran back to his half, apologizing as he went. When he looked back towards the edge of the pitch Ian had already gone.

The Stallions went on to lose the game by four goals to one – Leyton were just too good – but at the end of the game, instead of being rude, the Leyton players ran straight over to Jerome.

'You're a proper baller,' said one of them.

'Yeah, if you ever get tired of playing for them, you know where to come.'

Manny laughed and clapped Jerome on the back. 'Hands off, he's ours.'

'You heard the man,' said Jerome.

'But seriously,' said Leyton's captain, 'this was the best game your lot have given us. And you –'

'Jerome,' said Jerome.

'Jerome, you were a different class. I've played with a few people who are playing for big teams. You're better than them.'

Jerome smiled but inside he felt a little sad. 'Thanks so much,' he said. 'And best of luck in the tournament. I don't see anyone beating you.'

He shook hands with the captain and then walked back to the dressing room, where everyone cheered as soon as he walked in.

'Great team effort,' said Steve. 'We worked really hard out there. I know we lost but I'm proud of all of you. 'And,' he added, 'what a lovely goal, Jerome. Glad to see that you have a new fan.'

'I wish we had recorded it!' said Manny. 'It would have been the goal of the season! Wrighty would have talked about it on *Match of the Day*!'

'OK, now calm down,' Steve said with a laugh. He

turned to the board and rubbed off the team tactics that he had drawn there. 'See you all on Wednesday for training.'

Jerome helped Steve fold away the kit and put the footballs back into the bags, so he was one of the last people to leave the dressing room. By the time he was out on the main road, he was all by himself, but his sadness at defeat had been slowly replaced by joy. *Ian Wright likes the way I play football*, he thought. *Ian Wright!*

4

UNCLE RAY'S

That afternoon, Jerome looked in the bathroom mirror and shook his head. His hair had grown so big and bushy that a small bird could hide in it. It was the end of half-term holiday soon, and he could not go back to school looking like this: if he did, the teasing would be unbelievable. And he knew who would tease him the most – it would definitely be Jack MacKenzie.

It was as if MacKenzie could smell whenever Jerome was having a bad day. If Jerome walked through school feeling sad, then he knew he would bump into MacKenzie in the corridor. Even some of the teachers were afraid of him. There was a story that, at his last school, MacKenzie got so angry with another boy that he threw him in a skip and the boy was stuck in there for two days. No one knew if the story was true because no one dared to ask MacKenzie.

No, thought Jerome. He had to get a haircut, for sure.

'Mum, I need to go to the barber's,' he said, walking into the kitchen.

Stephanie glanced up from her lunch. 'You've got that right,' she said.

'*Mum.*'

'Sorry, Jerome! Only joking. But it has got a bit wild up there. I would cut it for you, but I've got an extra shift tonight.'

She nodded towards the living room, where Larry was sleeping. 'I would ask him to do it, only it's not really his thing.'

No surprises there, thought Jerome. 'I wanted to get it cut at Diamond D,' he said, 'but I didn't book an appointment, and the queues are going to be huge.' Diamond D was the best place to get your hair cut in Hackney – you had to get there early, though. That was where many of the local MCs got their trims done, and where you could get the latest styles that all the top footballers were wearing.

'How about Uncle Ray's?' said Stephanie.

'Uncle Ray's? No way!' wailed Jerome. 'That's where all the old men go. They're going to make me look like a granddad.' He could already imagine the joy on MacKenzie's face.

'Oh come on; it's not that bad. Ray knows what he's

doing. He's been running that place for forty years.'

'Yes,' grumbled Jerome, 'and no one I know has ever been in there.'

Stephanie regarded her son impatiently. 'Jerome, you're just being silly – and a little bit rude. Ray is a very nice man. Please make sure you say hello from me when you go over there. In fact, that reminds me.' She stood and went over to the cupboard, from which she took two plastic tubs, and then began to fill them with some of the food she had made that morning.

'What are you putting in there?' asked Jerome, suspicious.

'Some ackee and saltfish. Ray loves it.'

'But there won't be any left for me!'

'Jerome!' said Stephanie. 'What has got into you today? There is always some food left for you.'

'There wasn't last time,' he muttered, thinking of the chicken that Larry ate.

'What did you say?'

'Nothing,' said Jerome quickly. He took the tubs from his mother's hand. 'I'm sure he will be overjoyed with these. I might even ask him for a discount on the haircut.'

'Don't you dare!'

'Just joking, Mum! Just joking. See you later. Love you.'

'Love you, Jerome.'

***

Uncle Ray's was a twenty-minute walk across town, fifteen if you walked quickly, but Jerome was not in a hurry. He slouched along the high street, hood up, feeling sorry for himself. All his friends were going to be hanging out at Diamond D, and he was going to be hanging out with their dads and uncles. *What a boring way to spend the last day of my holidays*, he thought. Just when he believed his day could not get any worse, it did.

'Hey, Jerome! Jerome, is that you?'

Oh no, he thought. It was Aaron's friend – the one who stressed him out when she looked at him. She had her hair up in a bun, and she was wearing a black tracksuit and trainers, like she was on her way to the gym.

'Hi, Michelle,' he said. He couldn't say anything else and he didn't know why.

'Where are you going?'

'I'm off to get my hair cut,' he said. He pulled his hood down even more, so she couldn't see what a mess his hair was.

'Then why are you going that way? Diamond D is in the other direction.'

'I'm going to Uncle Ray's,' he said.

'Oh.'

'What's wrong with that?'

'Nothing's wrong with Uncle Ray's,' she said. 'It's just that a lot of us are meeting at Diamond. Amira and Aaron will be there.' She paused. 'I'll be there.'

'Oh,' said Jerome.

Michelle waited a little but Jerome didn't speak.

'Well, I hope you have a nice day,' she said, after a while.

'You too, Michelle,' he said. As he walked away, he felt that she was still looking at him, and when he looked back, she was. He smiled at her, she smiled back, and he carried on.

After a short while Jerome took a left turn off the main road and down a side street. The first thing he saw, fixed to the wall next to him, was a bright red poster carrying words in white:

UNCLE RAY'S, RIGHT THIS WAY
HACKNEY'S FINEST HAIRCUTS SINCE 1977

As he went past the poster, towards the end of the street, he heard music coming from the open door of the furthest shop. But it wasn't any of the music he or his friends listened to. It reminded him of the songs that his dad used to put on the stereo at home, when he and Jerome's mum would dance in the middle of the living room after a long day at work. He walked faster, to get closer to the sound, and to get closer to the memory of his parents dancing. Some of the singer's words floated out into the street, and as Jerome heard them he felt happier, calmer.

As he stepped into the doorway, a grinning and smartly dressed man greeted him at once. He wore dark blue trousers, a plain white shirt with his sleeves rolled up to his elbows, and a dark blue apron. He had a short grey beard and a short grey Afro on top of his head: there was a small parting cut through the left side of his hair, which looked like a path through a cornfield. He was humming along to the song that was playing in the barbershop, and he looked glad that Jerome was enjoying it too.

'You know who this is?'

'No,' said Jerome.

'You should,' said the man. 'It's the great Barrington Levy. Magical voice!' He looked at the bag in Jerome's hand. 'I see Stephanie has a delivery for me.'

'You knew I was coming?' said Jerome.

'Of course!' said the man. 'She gave me a call earlier. She said, "Ray, make sure my boy gets one of those modern cuts." I promised her you would be just fine.'

Now Jerome was grinning too. He didn't know why, but he felt like he could trust this man at once.

'Come inside, come inside,' said Ray. 'Plenty of empty chairs this afternoon – just take your pick. It's a very quiet day in here, just me and the selecta.' He waved towards someone at the back of the shop, a bald man in a black sweater and big black headphones, who was standing behind a DJ booth. The man was leaning forward over the record player, getting ready to change the vinyl LP that was playing for another one.

'You have a DJ playing records while you cut people's hair?' asked Jerome.

Ray laughed. 'Of course I do! Where do you think those boys at Diamond D got the idea from?' He waited while Jerome took his hood off, and then inspected his head. 'Ah, you've got a lot on top there. Even more than your dad.'

'You used to cut my dad's hair?' said Jerome.

'I did indeed!' said Ray. 'But only once or twice a year.' The music stopped and Ray looked towards the back of the shop. 'Selecta, where are the tunes?'

'Sorry, Ray, I'm just looking for some Freddie McGregor,' said the man, and then he looked up and made eye contact with Jerome.

'Oh my God!' said the man.

'Oh my God,' said Jerome.

'You're joking!' shouted the man. 'You're that boy who scored that wonder goal on Hackney Marshes last week!'

'You're … you're Ian Wright!' cried Jerome. Before he knew what was happening, Ian had already run up to him, and was squeezing his hand in greeting.

'What – what are you doing in here?'

'When I was playing for Arsenal, I used to come here and get some of my trims done,' said Ian. 'That's when me and Ray became mates, so I started to come here all the time. Now,' he said, patting the top of his head, 'I don't need haircuts so much any more. But Ray is such a good friend that I come in here just to relax and play tunes. So I'm his official Sunday afternoon DJ.' Then he pointed at Jerome and smiled. 'But that's not important. I want to talk about *you*. Your goal was amazing! How did you do that?'

'I just –' Jerome stopped. *Wait,* he thought, *Ian Wright wants to know how I score goals?* 'Why are you asking me?'

'Because I want to know what you were thinking,' said Ian.

'Go on,' said Ray gently. 'You can tell him.'

'Well,' said Jerome, 'I saw how Leyton were playing in the first half. And they were bullying us, a bit. They were saying mean things. And I thought: my team needs something to make them believe.'

'A big moment?' asked Ian.

'Yes,' said Jerome. 'A big moment. You know how when you score a goal that's so good, it changes the whole match? One where it makes your team feel you can do anything? I needed to score a goal like that.'

Ian smiled. 'I know just what you mean.'

'So the ball dropped to me and I saw their captain coming, and I thought, I need to score this goal when he is standing near me. Because he needs to feel that me and my team have more power than him. He needs to see it. And I wanted their goalkeeper to feel like we could score at any time. That whenever we shot the ball, there was danger. So I thought, I need to shoot from here. Right now, when we are in this pitch, right in the middle of the Marshes, where everyone can see it. I have to send a message. And that's why I scored that goal.'

Ian rubbed his forehead slowly, as if he was trying to arrange his thoughts in there.

'This is going to sound so strange,' he said. 'I'm sorry, I didn't even get your name –'

'Jerome.'

'Jerome,' said Ian, 'this will sound strange but when I was watching you play, I thought, this boy sees the game the way I do. Ask Ray. I came in here last Sunday and I told him, Ray there's this kid on the Marshes… I just watched him for five minutes then I had to leave, but I'm still thinking about it, hours later. Just the way he was fighting for every ball. He was so intense. He was playing just like me.'

'It's true,' said Ray. 'I haven't seen him talk like that about a player in years.'

'Why aren't you at an academy or something?' asked Ian. 'Arsenal, at least? Everyone should be after you.'

Jerome didn't reply. Instead, he slowly and nervously took a seat, staring ahead of him into the mirror.

'Ray,' he said quietly, 'I would like a really simple one if that's OK. Short on top, with a drop fade, please.'

Ray picked up the clippers from the nearby tray. 'Sure thing, Jerome,' he said, and began to cut.

'It's difficult to talk about,' said Jerome.

Ian sat down into an empty chair next to Jerome, and he got ready to listen. 'You don't have to if you don't want to,' he said gently.

After a few more seconds of silence in the barbershop, Jerome spoke.

'It's fine.' He breathed out, hard. 'A few years ago, my football was going really well. My dad would take me to training, to my games. After a while all the clubs were interested in me. Arsenal, Manchester City, Manchester United, Liverpool. They invited me to trials. And then, the week before I had all my trials, my dad died.' He took a long breath, as if he were about to go underwater. 'I went and did my trials but all I could think about was Dad just lying there all alone before they found him, dead on the floor. And I never played so badly in all my life. I missed every chance. One of the coaches was shocked because he had heard I was so good and when I turned up, I heard him say to his mate, "It is as if no one even taught this boy how to kick." And they all sent me home and I was so unhappy that I didn't play football again for a year. And now I play for Hackney Stallions. I know they are not the best team in the world, but they are good people and I'm just trying to get my confidence back.'

'Oh, Jerome,' said Ian. He put a hand on Jerome's shoulder. 'Thank you so much for telling me that.'

Jerome felt himself starting to cry and he put his sleeve to his eyes to stop his tears, but Ray had already given him a tissue.

'No need to spoil your nice clothes, young man,' he said.

'Do you still want to be a footballer?' asked Ian.

Jerome turned towards Ian. 'More than anything in the world,' he said.

'Good,' said Ian. 'There's a long way to go, but you have to have the dream. Always.'

He stood up and walked back to the DJ table. 'First I'm going to put on some music,' he said, 'and then we are going to talk about your dream of playing football. We are going to talk about how you can get there. How does that sound?'

'That sounds perfect,' said Jerome. He was already wondering what his friends would think. *Ian Wright!*

'What kind of music do you listen to?' asked Ian.

'J Hus, mostly,' said Jerome. 'And Little Simz. And Stormzy.'

'All very good,' said Ian. 'But now I'm going to play some of the people who inspired them. Some of the older stuff. What do you know about a guy called Kirk Franklin?'

Jerome shrugged.

'Very well. Some Kirk coming right up,' said Ian, sliding a vinyl record from the case beneath the table.

'Ian,' said Ray, 'while you're over there, could you get me a coffee? Milk, two sugars.' Ray looked at Jerome in the mirror, and grinned. 'In fact – two of those, please.'

'Oh really,' said Ian. 'So now I'm the coffee boy?'

'Yes, you are!' yelled Ray. 'Now hurry up, young man! We haven't got all day.' The three of them laughed, and the beautiful music began to fill the air.

5

IN BRIGHTON

For the whole of the next week, Jerome could not stop smiling. He, Ray and Ian had chatted for hours at the barbershop, and at the end they had agreed to meet up again every two weeks, to see how Jerome was doing with his football. He didn't tell his mum or Larry or his friends that he had made friends with Ian – he just wanted to keep it for himself for now, as his happy secret. But everyone could tell that something good had happened to him. At home, when Larry was very mean to him, he was more polite than usual. At school he arrived early to every class, including for the subjects that he didn't really enjoy, and he didn't get sad if he got a bad mark in a test; he just asked how he could get better. He didn't run through the building, even when he was in a hurry; he just left the way and allowed everyone else to walk past first. He was being so nice that even the people who didn't like him had started to notice it.

'Oi, Jerome,' called MacKenzie, as Jerome walked towards him in the corridor. 'What's wrong with you?'

'What do you mean?' asked Jerome.

'Your whole energy this week, it's weird.'

'My energy?'

'Stop being clever,' said MacKenzie. 'Normally when I come at you, you're different. Like, I say something, and you get angry. But this week you're more... I don't know. Stupid.'

Jerome faked ignorance. 'Stupid?' he repeated.

'Yeah, you don't answer back. You don't react. You just stand there with that silly grin on your face.'

'Now, MacKenzie,' said Mrs Matthews, their chemistry teacher. She had heard the conversation as she approached, and she was frowning. 'That's not a very pleasant thing to say.'

'Sorry, miss,' said MacKenzie at once. Mrs Matthews was the kindest teacher in the school and so he wanted her to like him.

'It is not me you should apologize to,' she said, and nodded towards Jerome.

MacKenzie pouted. 'Sorry, Jerome.'

'No worries, MacKenzie,' said Jerome calmly, which made MacKenzie even more angry.

Mrs Matthews looked amused. 'Good,' she said. 'Now,

MacKenzie, please can you help me carry these textbooks to class?'

'Of course, miss,' said MacKenzie.

'And, Jerome,' said Mrs Matthews, as the two of them walked away, 'I love your new haircut!'

***

Soon enough, Sunday arrived again; the day Jerome looked forward to all week, but this week most of all. All he could think about was what Ian had told him in the barbershop. *The next time you go out on that pitch,* said Ian, *that's when your dream starts. That's where you have to show them who you really are. You need to play every game like you're already famous, like you're already the best in the world. That's who you need to be.*

That morning, Jerome woke up before the dawn, before his mum, before Larry. He was playing in a regional six-a-side tournament for Hackney Methodist, his local church, all the way down near the south coast. It was a two-hour journey, and so they had to set off very early. When Jerome got to the church, the sun was only just starting to gaze between the buildings.

'Hey,' said Reverend Benjamin, as Jerome walked up to the minibus. 'Very glad you could make it!' He shook his hand and patted him hard on the back. 'Long time, no see.'

'I'm sorry,' said Jerome. He had not been at church very much recently. He used to go every Sunday with his mum, but now he missed most of the services to play football instead.

'You are welcome back anytime, you know,' said Reverend Benjamin. As he spoke, they both heard a rumbling at the back of the minibus, then a groan.

'Ow! Micah, you woke me up!'

'So what? Jerome's here!'

'You're joking?'

'Oh my days!'

Reverend Benjamin rolled his eyes. 'Look at the fuss you've caused,' he said.

'Who's in there?' asked Jerome.

'Oh, the usual crew,' said Reverend Benjamin. He opened the front passenger door for Jerome, the last seat left on the bus, then walked back round to the driver's side. As Jerome sat down, he felt several hands pat him on his shoulders, as his friends reached forward to greet him.

'Jerome!' said Izzy. 'It's been months, my guy.'

'I'm sorry,' replied Jerome. 'I've been busy.' As soon as he said that he regretted it.

'You're too busy for church, too busy for God?' said Ty. 'Wow. Must be big work.'

'Jerome, busy making moves! Listen to this man,' cackled Ikenna.

Jerome was going to come back with a quick reply, but then he stopped, and put his hands up in surrender. These boys were just too fast.

'They missed you, Jerome,' said Reverend Benjamin. He smiled and started the engine.

As they drove down towards Brighton, Jerome gazed out of the window and thought of all the great times he had had on church trips. Every couple of months, Reverend Benjamin and the worshippers would hire a coach and go somewhere far outside London, to visit a theme park or a beach or an old castle. It was always a chance for people to get away from their troubles and just spend some time walking around and being happy. The best thing was always the long ride home, when everyone but the driver was falling asleep, their minds full of happy memories from the day.

The blue road signs flew by – Brighton, 37 miles; Brighton, 36 miles – and Jerome remembered what Ian had told him. *Just go out there and don't change a thing. Just play your game, be natural. The worst thing you can do in football is to push too hard. Don't force it. And enjoy it.*

'Jerome,' said Reverend Benjamin. 'Jerome.'

'Sorry,' said Jerome. 'I was just getting my head ready for the tournament.'

'Oh, I'm not worried about that,' said Reverend Benjamin. 'I just wanted to know how things were at home.'

'It's not my home,' replied Jerome. 'It's just a place where I sleep in the evenings.'

'Oh,' said Reverend Benjamin. 'So Larry is still not being nice. How is he doing?'

Jerome shrugged, annoyed. 'Who cares about Larry?'

'Larry behaves like he does because he is not happy with his own life,' said Reverend Benjamin.

'Then why does he take it out on me?'

'Because he is not strong enough to carry his own pain. So he has to drop it on everyone else.'

'He's a man and he acts like the biggest kid in the flat.'

'It must be so frustrating.'

'It's worse than that. And what do you expect me to do? Just turn the other cheek like in the Bible?'

They stared at the road ahead for a while.

'I'm sorry,' said Jerome. 'He just makes me so angry.'

'It won't be like this for ever,' said Reverend Benjamin.

'How do you know that?'

'Everyone in this bus knows that. We all believe in you.'

'Yeah, Jerome!' shouted Samuel, who had been listening quietly to everything.

'Jackson! Jackson! Jackson!' chanted his friends. As they drove on down the motorway, the minibus filled with the song of his name.

'Shut up, you guys,' said Jerome, but he never wanted them to stop.

As soon as Jerome arrived in Brighton, he knew it was going to be a special day. They were playing on a hill that looked down over the town and the beach, where the sea stretched away out of sight. The sun sparkled over the water, and the seagulls chattered to each other as they flew in wide circles overhead. The grass had been cut the day before and it smelled as sweet as fresh apples, and the newly painted touchlines gleamed bright white.

On the hill there were six small pitches side by side, around which stood hundreds of people from churches all over the south-east of England, there to support their teams. There was a long row of tables laid out a few yards from the pitches, which carried trays of food for lunch and dinner. And then there was a separate table, on which stood a tall silver trophy, the reward for winning that day's tournament. *That's ours*, thought Jerome. *We are taking that cup home.*

The tournament had thirty-two teams, split into eight groups of four. The winner of each group went through to the quarter-finals, and Jerome's team did that easily. He hadn't played with them for years, but they were still such good friends that it didn't matter: they knew how to play together. Ty in goal. Izzy ran the defence, simple. Ikenna, Jacob and Femi to control midfield; Andy and Micah on the bench; and Jerome up top, always. They won each of their three group games, 3–0, 3–1 and 5–1, with Jerome scoring six times. The quarter-final was easy too, and here they had a 4–1 win: two goals from Jerome, one from Andy, one from Izzy, which they celebrated like it was the World Cup. The semi-final was tougher, and their opponents went 1–0 up, but Jerome scored his team's first goal, Femi got the second, and, a few seconds before the final whistle, Jerome got the third. That meant they were in the final, against Angel of Hastings, and they were given a half-hour break before the big game.

Jerome lay on his back on the grass and smiled up at the sky. *This is perfect*, he thought. *Maybe me and Mum could move down here in the middle of the night, before Larry wakes up, and just stay in a flat by the beach, and then I could come up here every weekend and score goals on this hill.* He looked across at the water, at the sea that went on for ever, and he had never felt so free.

'Young man!'

Jerome looked up to see an angry man glaring down at him. 'You are not playing in that final,' said the man, jabbing a finger in his direction.

Jerome stood up at once. 'What – what's this about?' he asked.

'I don't believe you go to Hackney Methodist Church,' said the man. 'You're too good. I think the Reverend brought you here just so you could win this tournament for them.'

'What?' said Jerome. 'You think I'm a ringer?'

'Yes!' spluttered the man. 'I think you're a cheat.'

Jerome waited a few seconds for the man's breathing to slow down.

'Have you ever had a hard time being religious?' Jerome asked. 'Like some days you prayed and prayed but nothing seemed to change?'

'What has that got to do with it?' said the man.

'Everything,' said Jerome. He pointed across at his

friends, who were getting ready for the final. 'These boys from the church are like brothers to me. But I haven't seen them in too long. You know when you make a mistake and you don't put it right at once, and then more and more time goes past, and you think it's too late?'

'Yes – yes,' said the man, looking confused. 'I suppose so.'

'Well, I felt like that until today. I don't go to church as much as I used to. But today has shown me how much my friends from Hackney Methodist are there for me. Even when I'm not always there for them. It's been a bit like coming home, you know?'

'Oh,' said the man. And then he said, 'I'm sorry.'

'It's OK,' said Jerome.

'I just so badly wanted to win,' said the man. 'And I get too competitive at times. My son is in the final. And I saw you playing in the earlier rounds, and I thought, if we play them then that Jackson boy is going to be trouble. All the parents were talking about you. That goal you scored when you went past two players and put it in the bottom corner – my goodness. I'm a Manchester United fan and it reminded me of what Ian Wright did to us in that cup final. You move just like him.'

'Sorry, what?' said Jerome.

'You know, Ian Wright. In the 1990 FA Cup final.' The man looked embarrassed. 'Oh no – you weren't even born then.'

'No, no, it's fine. I mean, that's really nice,' said Jerome.

'It's just funny you should mention him. That's such a kind thing to say.'

The stranger shrugged. 'I say what I see.'

The referee blew the whistle. 'Five minutes till kick-off!' she said. 'Captains, come in for the coin toss, please.'

As the teams began to jog towards the pitch, Jerome turned to the man. 'Good to chat with you,' he said.

'Ha, yes, it was in the end,' the man replied.

'Best of luck to your son,' said Jerome.

'Go easy on him, please!' said the man. 'He's the goalkeeper.'

In the final, Hackney Methodist beat Angel of Hastings by four goals to nil. Jerome scored all four of them, and the last one was the most beautiful of all. Izzy saw him next to the touchline, just inside his own half and facing his own goal and hit the ball very hard along the grass to him. Three Angel players sprinted towards Jerome, but just before they got to him Jerome touched the ball with the back of his heel and then suddenly ran back towards his own goal. The three Angel players, taken by surprise, ran through the space Jerome had just left and off the pitch, almost knocking over a member of the crowd. Jerome turned, knocked the ball forward with one touch from his left foot, and now he was alone with the goalkeeper. He raised his right foot as if he was about to shoot, then brought it down fast, and stopped it on top of the ball. The goalkeeper dived away to his left, and Jerome rolled the ball into the empty net. When he turned around, everyone was clapping – even the angry man from before the game, who was now shaking his head and smiling. 'Too good,' he called out. 'Too good.'

The rest of the day was perfect. When Hackney Methodist went to collect their trophy from the winner's table, they didn't just send their captain, they all went up together, and each of them had a hand on the cup as they lifted it. 'This was a real team effort,' said Reverend Benjamin. 'Just as it should be. Everyone played their part.' The team sang songs in the minibus all the way back from Brighton. Jerome was so happy when he got off the bus that he didn't even notice the cold.

'Thanks very much for joining us, Jerome,' said Reverend Benjamin, as they stood in the car park.

'It was amazing,' said Jerome. 'It was good to get the team back together.'

'I wish we saw you more often,' said Reverend Benjamin.

'Me too,' said Jerome. 'It's just…'

'I know,' said Reverend Benjamin. 'Just remember – we are always here for you. And we are always with you.'

'Thank you so much,' said Jerome.

Reverend Benjamin watched him walk away. *God bless you, Jerome,* he thought, *and good luck.*

6

IJEOMA'S HOUSE

A few evenings later, when Larry was out drinking with his friends, Jerome walked into the living room where his mum was watching television.

'Mum,' he announced, 'I want to take you for a meal as a treat. I've been saving up.'

Stephanie looked at him, surprised.

'Why?'

'Just because. Does there need to be a reason? I just want to say thank you.'

Stephanie frowned at Jerome. 'You've been acting very strangely recently. And what if I don't want to go out? What if I just want to rest after work?'

'Mum, when you are at home you always rest. So... let's go.'

'Oh, now my own son is ordering me around?'

Jerome didn't say anything. He just leaned back against the frame of the door and crossed his arms, just like his mum always did when she didn't want to argue any more.

Stephanie laughed. 'So it's like that?'

'Yes, Mum,' said Jerome, 'it's like that. I'll let you get ready. Just knock on my bedroom door when you're done.'

An hour later Stephanie knocked on Jerome's door, and he stepped out into the hallway. He was wearing his best outfit, the one he normally put on for church: blue blazer, white shirt, black trousers, black shoes. 'Look at you!' she said. 'Aren't you smart!' She was wearing a long dark green dress and green plimsolls. For the first time in months, she was wearing her hair down, and as she moved her curls bounced over her shoulders.

'Where are we going?' she asked. She looked at her hair anxiously in the hallway mirror. 'I look terrible.'

'No, Mum, you look great,' said Jerome. He held her light blue denim jacket behind her so she could put both of her arms into it, then he waited for her to button it up before he opened the door. 'You look lovely. Sometimes you say such mean things about yourself.'

'I'm sorry,' she said. 'It's just that I don't get to go out very much any more. Larry is always so busy. And when he is home, he just wants to eat and relax.'

They walked down the stairs together, out into the car park and then left, past the railway.

'I haven't been this way in a while,' said Stephanie. 'Are you sure this is the right way? There's nothing down here but car repairs.'

'There's a new Nigerian place here,' said Jerome. 'Ikenna said I should check it out.'

'Ikenna from church?'

'Yes.'

'You should go to Hackney Methodist more,' said Stephanie. 'It's good for you.'

Jerome didn't want to argue so he said nothing. They crossed the road and turned down a quiet street.

'Are you sure there's a restaurant here?' asked Stephanie.

'Very sure,' said Jerome. They came to a building on the corner of the street, with a glass window all along one side. There was a thick brown curtain against the window, with a cosy glow of light spilling around its edges.

'Here we are,' said Jerome, 'this is Ijeoma's House.'

'It actually looks like someone's house,' said Stephanie, as they stepped inside.

It was only a small restaurant, with room for four tables, each of which could seat four people. It was empty apart from the cook, who was shuffling about in the kitchen, and the waiter, who rushed to meet Jerome and Stephanie as soon as they entered. 'Please, please,' he said, handing them a menu each. 'Sit wherever you like.'

'Thank you,' said Jerome, as they took the table nearest

to the window. 'We are just waiting for one more.'

'A surprise guest?' said Stephanie. 'Jerome, you are being very mysterious today.'

Jerome smiled, enjoying himself. Just as he did so, the door rattled again, and Ian came in, looked about, spotted them and walked to their table. The waiter was so surprised to see Ian there that, at first, he forgot to offer him a menu.

'Here's my new friend,' said Jerome to Stephanie. 'I thought you might like to meet him. He's been really helpful to me.'

'Hi, my name's Ian,' said Ian, offering his hand to Stephanie.

'Stephanie,' she said, shaking it. 'And of course I know who you are. I read all about you. How it took you ages to make it as a footballer. How things were so difficult for you at home growing up. My husband Martin had so much respect for you.' Stephanie coughed into her fist, the way she always did when she was a little bit nervous.

'So, Jerome,' she said, 'that explains why you've been acting so differently these last few days. Your new famous friend.'

Jerome's jaw dropped open. 'You know him? Mum, you don't even like football that much!'

'Jerome!' said Stephanie. 'Everyone's seen Ian play football.'

'Well, I'm a lot slower these days,' said Ian.

Stephanie laughed. 'Aren't we all,' she said, relaxing a bit.

60

'You know those times when you have so much work that the week just goes on for ever?' Ian nodded. 'This has been one of those weeks.' Stephanie stretched out her legs as far as she could under the table. 'I'm so tired that I wish I could eat lying down.'

'I know that feeling,' said Ian. 'The hardest time I had at work was long before I was a footballer. I was working as a plasterer, and one weekend our team had to do the whole floor of this office block. One of those new buildings in Canary Wharf, the ones they seem to put up in about five minutes. My back was so stiff. But Stephanie, the worst thing about it was the smell. You would not believe it but for the next two weeks all I could smell was the chemicals from the plaster. Even when I was eating, my nostrils were full of it!'

'If you ever have that problem again,' said the waiter, 'you can try the pepper soup. It is strong enough to break through anything.'

'Sounds like my kind of challenge,' said Ian. 'One for me, please.' He looked over at Jerome. 'You in?'

'Sure thing,' said Jerome. 'Mum?'

'Oh, why not,' said Stephanie. 'Pepper soup for three, please.'

Twenty minutes later they were all sitting back in their chairs, sweating and giggling, finishing and refilling their glasses of water every couple of minutes.

'Oh my goodness,' said Stephanie. 'I don't actually think I can feel my mouth any more.'

'This was not pepper soup,' said Ian, 'this was fire soup.'

Jerome was about to say something, but then he stopped and coughed, his eyes filled up with water from the heat of the food, and they all started laughing again.

'Oh my gosh,' he said, as the waiter smiled with pride.

'So Ian,' said Stephanie, 'how did you and my son meet?'

'It was complete luck,' said Ian. 'The other day. I was at my mate's barbershop – you know Uncle Ray's, near Cambridge Heath?'

'You know Ray? I love Ray!' said Stephanie.

'Yeah, me and Ray go way back!' said Ian. 'I was just in there and Jerome walks in – and I think, oh my God, it's that guy from Hackney Marshes!' He paused. 'Wait, Jerome didn't tell you?'

'Tell me what?' said Stephanie at once. She sounded worried. 'He wasn't in trouble?'

'No, no,' said Ian quickly. 'Not at all. The opposite. Jerome scored a goal so good on Hackney Marshes that everyone stopped and cheered. Unbelievable strike. He hit it from way, way out – and he didn't even seem like he was trying to hit it that hard, but it just flew. It was like a harpoon.'

Stephanie looked at her son but couldn't talk; she was speechless with pride.

'Watching him,' said Ian, 'I thought – this boy plays just like me. Same style, same spirit. Maybe better.'

'Better than you!' said Stephanie.

'Maybe,' said Ian. 'Very few people believed in me for a long time. I nearly didn't make it. And that's why I wanted to talk to Jerome, and to talk to you.'

Stephanie raised her eyebrows. She looked at Jerome, then back at Ian.

'I've got sons of my own in football,' said Ian. 'And I wouldn't say this if I didn't mean it, but I think your son is good enough to make it. Not just to be a footballer, but to be a top footballer. But he's not quite there yet. I don't think he believes in himself yet.'

Jerome had his head down over his bowl and Stephanie put her hand on his. 'It's OK, Jerome.'

'Absolutely,' said Ian. 'It's OK and that is why I'm here. Because I want to help you and I want to help your mum.'

'I told him about Dad dying before my football trials,' said Jerome.

'Wow, he told you that?' said Stephanie. Ian nodded.

'Ian, you know when I celebrated that time,' said Jerome. 'Every single goal I score, I always count out the number fifteen with my hand. I do that because my dad died on the fourteenth day of the month. So when I count to fifteen it's like my dad is alive for one more day.'

Ian didn't speak. There were tears in his eyes.

'Your dad would want you to make it, Jerome,' he said, after a little while. 'And he would want you to know you are good enough.'

'I have to go to the bathroom,' said Jerome, and he went to the back of the restaurant so fast that he was almost running. But he was not quick enough for Ian not to see that he was crying too.

'Well, this got very emotional,' said Stephanie, dabbing a napkin around the corners of her eyes. 'He'd never told me about the goal celebration before.'

'Jerome told me how hard you work for him,' said Ian.

'It's very tough for him. Very tough,' said Stephanie. 'Sometimes I worry I make it even harder for him. My boyfriend Larry moved in with us, but he and Jerome just don't get on. I thought it might even help Jerome to have a man at home ... but it's been the opposite. Sometimes it's just so tense and I can't stand it. They think I don't notice, but they are always fighting.'

Ian nodded.

'I just don't understand,' she continued. 'Larry was so lovely when I met him. And I think I thought if he fell in love with me then he would love Jerome too. But I was so wrong.' She took a long drink from her glass. 'Larry has not had an easy road either. I think that's why he is always having a go at Jerome. When he looks at Jerome, he sees someone who is wasting his chance.'

'Jerome will get another chance,' Ian said, 'and he won't waste it. We will all see to that.' He asked the waiter for a pen and paper, and wrote down his number, passing it to Stephanie. 'You are doing your bit for him and I'll try and do mine. Give me a text any time if you need to chat.'

'But you must be so busy,' said Stephanie.

'No one is busier than you,' said Ian. 'You are trying to bring up a kid basically by yourself and that is the hardest thing anyone can do. Please, get in touch with me any time.'

'Thank you so much,' said Stephanie. She folded the piece of paper with Ian's number on it and put it in her jacket pocket. As she did that, Jerome strolled back to the table.

'Did you miss me?' he asked.

'You wish!' said Stephanie.

'Look at this guy,' said Ian, shaking his head and smiling. 'He eats one pepper soup and he thinks he is the king.'

'Ready to order your main course?' said the waiter.

'Yes,' said Jerome. He hesitated, looking anxious and a little bit scared. 'But please – please – nothing hot this time!'

Everyone except Jerome burst out laughing, and then Jerome started laughing too. For the first time in a long while, it looked like things might turn out just fine.

7

JEROME STARTS TO RUN

Jerome's phone buzzed in his pocket, telling him that he had a new text message. It was from Aaron.

```
Hey stranger
```

```
                    What do you mean,
                      stranger? I only
                    saw you last week
```

```
Yeah and since you met
Michelle you turned
into a ghost. You
disappeared again. Why
do you always do that
when it comes to girls?
```

What do you mean?

Allow it Jerome.
I know you

OK it's true. I don't know what it is about girls. They just make me nervous. Not all of them. Just ones like Michelle

Ones that you like?

Aaron did you actually want anything?

Hey, relax! What you up to later?

Not much, why?

Would be cool if we could hang out.
About nine.

Where?

Canning Avenue.

The posh road? What you
going up there for?

I've got some mates
up there. Come along,
it'll be jokes.

Ah I don't know
if I will Aaron.

Don't be lame,
Jerome. I promise I
won't scare you by
bringing Michelle.

Aaron.

Just joking! See
you later?

Sure thing. See
you later.

Safe.

That evening, Jerome put on his jacket, and went to meet Aaron. As usual on a Saturday night, Hackney was very busy, so it took Jerome a long time to get through the crowds. *So many people!* thought Jerome. It seemed like everyone in London had come to his area to go to a bar or a club or a restaurant. He felt his phone buzzing in his jacket pocket again and took it out.

'Where are you?' asked Aaron. 'I've tried calling you three times!'

'I'm on my way,' said Jerome.

Aaron tutted. 'You forget who your real friends are.'

'What do you mean by that?' Jerome asked.

'Can you get a move on?' said Aaron. 'We need you here for nine.'

'Hey, calm down,' said Jerome. 'I thought we were going to have a relaxed evening. What's the rush?'

'It won't be relaxed if you're not on time.' Aaron sounded really annoyed, nervous even. 'Twenty-three Canning Avenue. Don't be late.'

'OK, OK!' said Jerome. He was feeling stressed now. 'I'll be there! Aaron, do you need—' But Aaron had already hung up.

By the time Jerome got to the top of Canning Avenue, the sun had already set. It was one of the most expensive streets in Hackney, with several sports cars parked along the pavement. Some of the gardens were so big that you couldn't see to the end of them, even with the help of the lights from the street. Somewhere in there, at the back of the darkness, were huge houses. One of Jerome's friends delivered some food there once, and he said that when the front door opened it was like looking into a museum.

'Jerome. Over here. Jerome.' A boy's voice came towards him, quiet but angry. 'There you are. We needed you; you nearly let us down.' The speaker stepped out from behind a car. He wore an all-black tracksuit and trainers, his black puffer jacket zipped all the way up to his neck and his hood up.

'Who are you?' said Jerome. 'What's this? Who's "we"? Where's Aaron?'

The boy pointed towards the house in front of them. 'Him and Matt are in there. They will be out in a few minutes. We are meant to keep lookout.'

'Lookout for what?'

'You're not very sharp, are you? This family is always showing off – they have tons of luxury watches and jewellery lying around their house. So Matt and Aaron are in there cleaning them out and we are out here watching in case the police turn up.'

'But wait.' Jerome suddenly felt dizzy, like that time he had jumped in the swimming pool without taking a breath and his nose had filled up with water. 'There's no party? Aaron brought me here to help him steal stuff?' Jerome looked around at the houses and then at the empty street. He thought about all the years he had known Aaron. 'Why would he ask me to do this?'

'Because he says he can trust you and you are a quick runner and you can spot trouble a mile off.'

'But Aaron is the trouble here,' said Jerome. He looked towards the house then back again. No police cars in sight. 'Listen – I didn't get your name...'

'That's because I didn't give it to you,' said the boy, folding his arms. 'They know you; I don't. Don't want you snitching on me if you get caught.'

Jerome thought of his mum, working so hard to make sure they had a place to live, and then he thought of Ian, trying to give him a chance to achieve his dream ... and that was when he knew that he had to go.

'I'm out of here,' he said, and turned to leave, walking quickly towards the main road.

'Some friend you are,' said the boy. 'You'd better not grass us up!'

'Hey! You!' called another voice from about fifty metres away. To his shock, Jerome saw a group of four men in black jackets sprinting towards them. He saw them shove the boy against one of the cars, and fix handcuffs around his wrists. Police!

'There's another one! I'll get him!' shouted one of the officers, and he began to pursue Jerome.

Jerome started to run. He leaned forward and his toes hammered away at the pavement. He straightened his hands into blades and slashed away at the air. He opened his mouth wide and dragged the wind into his lungs. He had never run so fast; not even when he was chasing a pass from one of his teammates; not even when he was trying to catch the last train back from West London. This time he was running for his future, for his life! But when he looked over his shoulder he saw that the police officer was getting even closer, only thirty metres back now. *How is this man so fast?* wondered Jerome. *He is quicker than me, how do I get away from him? Think, Jerome, think!*

'Come back here!' yelled the officer. They were approaching the main road, and as they did so Jerome saw a huge and noisy crowd of people walking past the top of Canning Avenue. This was his chance! *Come on, Jerome*, he thought. *Just a few metres more!*

Jerome got to the corner of the street, and at the very last moment he swerved to his left – and then stopped at once, standing with his back to the wall. The police officer, by now running at full pelt, carried on round the corner, past where his quarry hid, and it took a couple of seconds before he realized that the boy he was pursuing had disappeared. In that time, Jerome had taken off his jacket and ducked into the crowd, so when the police officer looked back all he saw were dozens of pedestrians.

'Police!' shouted the officer desperately. 'Police!' But most people couldn't hear him over the noise of the shouting and the traffic, and by the time they did hear him Jerome had crossed the main road, turned down a narrow alleyway, and was gone.

***

As Jerome turned the key in the front door of his flat, he heard the television shouting from the living room. Stepping inside, he saw his mum's plimsolls and Larry's boots in the hallway, and he tiptoed past them to his bedroom, shutting and locking the door quietly behind him. He sat on his bed and checked his phone. No calls or text messages from Aaron – he hoped he would be OK. *Aaron*, he thought, *what were you doing?* Jerome turned the light off and lay on his back. He stayed like that for hours, the sweat drying to salt on his forehead, his breathing slowing, as he waited for the police to knock on the door any second. But they never did.

Jerome didn't hear from Aaron all weekend. He didn't dare call him in case the police picked up the phone instead. It wasn't until Monday, while waiting for lunch in the school canteen, that he found out what had happened to his friend. Two boys standing in front of him in the queue started talking about Aaron, and as they spoke Jerome stepped a little closer, while trying to pretend that he was not listening.

'Did you hear about Aaron?'

'Nah, what's that?'

'Him, Matt and Lorenzo got caught robbing some banker's house.'

'No way.'

'Yeah. On Saturday. Turns out they had done a bunch of houses and flats in the area already. Aaron was hiding the stuff at his girlfriend Amira's house. The police went there and found a load of it. They arrested Amira too.'

'Wow. Didn't think Aaron was into that.'

'Guess you never know. True, true. I spoke to Lorenzo's cousin – it's really bad. They are going to send them to a secure training unit.'

'They aren't so bad.'

'Not normally but they want to send them to that one down in Kent.'

'Oh my God.'

'Yeah, I know. Their lives are done. They are screwed.'

'Definitely.'

'The police said there was one other burglar, but he got away.'

'Oh yeah?'

'They couldn't find him. They said he was young, Black and quick.'

The boy laughed. 'Really?'

'No, just joking. But Aaron, Lorenzo and Matt didn't tell the police who he was.'

'Lucky guy.'

'Real talk.'

As the boys took their food and walked away to their table, Jerome realized just how close he had come to losing his dream. There was no way any major football club would touch a young boy who had just come out of jail for helping to rob houses. No way at all. That afternoon in class, he couldn't concentrate on his work. He was too busy thinking about Aaron, his friend for so many years, sitting in the back of a van on his way out of London, his life changed for ever. Poor, silly Aaron. What was he thinking? What was he doing? *Maybe*, thought Jerome, *I don't really know Aaron any more.*

That evening Jerome went straight to his room as soon as he got home. He looked out of the window and imagined that he was in a prison cell, staring down at the street outside, unable to leave. What if that officer had caught him? It had been so, so close.

He heard a knock on his door. Was that the police?

'Jerome. Jerome.' It was Larry – but his voice sounded different, a little softer. Jerome had never heard him use that voice before. 'Your mum is worried about you. This is the third night in a row you haven't eaten dinner. She just wants to know if you're OK.'

'Hey – yes, I'm fine, thanks. Thanks for checking, Larry.'

'Well maybe at least come out and show her yourself.' Now he sounded angrier, and Jerome hesitated. 'She has enough to worry about.'

Jerome was suddenly not so happy about leaving his room. But Larry was also right. His mum was out there, and she needed him. He rolled off his bed and to his feet, shuffled past a frowning Larry, and into the living room.

His mum was sitting in the armchair, exhausted again, her body barely moving as she watched the television. She looked up towards Jerome and as soon as he made eye contact with her, he burst into tears.

'Jerome, what is it?' she asked, stumbling to her feet and hugging him. 'What's happened?'

'Mum, I'm so sorry,' said Jerome. 'I'm so sorry.' Jerome was crying so hard that he was shaking now, and his mum held him as close as she could, cupping the back of his head in the palm of one of her hands. Larry stood awkwardly in the doorway, then went and sat in the middle of the sofa, ready to give his opinion.

After a few minutes Jerome stopped sobbing and rubbed his nose with his sleeve.

'I'm sorry,' he said, stepping back and blinking away the wetness in his eyes.

'Stop saying that,' said Larry. 'Out with it.'

'Larry!' said Stephanie.

'No, Mum,' said Jerome. 'Larry is right.' He waited for her to sit down and he stayed standing. 'You have probably heard they arrested Aaron.'

'Yes,' said Stephanie. 'His mum called me this afternoon. She and his dad are absolutely devastated.'

'Well,' said Jerome, 'they nearly arrested me too.'

'Jerome.'

She said his name with so much sadness in her voice that he nearly burst into tears again.

'I knew he was going to turn out like this,' said Larry. His sneer was back.

'It wasn't like that!' pleaded Jerome. 'Aaron told me to meet him on my way from work. I thought we were going to a party, but he wanted me to keep lookout for him while he was...' Jerome found it hard to finish the sentence, because he knew how bad it sounded.

'… While he was robbing a house.'

'Why did he want you there?'

'Because he said he could trust me.'

'Why?' asked Stephanie. 'You've done this before?'

'No, Mum, no! It's because him and me go way back as friends!'

'Jerome,' said Larry. 'Either you are a criminal or you are just stupid. You should be on your way to jail.'

Larry stood up and spat in the middle of the living room floor. Jerome and Stephanie didn't say anything. They just watched the white spit glistening until it dried into the carpet.

'You are throwing it all away,' said Larry. 'Like so many of you boys round here. You think you have nothing, but you have it all. Talent. A mum who actually cares. Three meals a day. A roof over your head.'

'I know I have all that,' said Jerome. 'That's why I—'

'Don't interrupt me!' roared Larry. 'I have been telling your mum this for months! The way you strut around the place. Too confident, like you are looking for trouble. Well, trouble has found you.'

Jerome was so stunned that he couldn't speak. He looked at his mum to defend him, but she wasn't saying anything; she couldn't even look at him.

Larry kept shouting but after a while Jerome couldn't hear him at all. All he could see was his mum sitting there, silent, with her head down, and all he could think was, *Where are you, Dad? We need you.*

8

THE NEXT STAGE

Jerome had never seen his mum so angry or so worried about him. For the next five weeks, she called him every afternoon to make sure that he was on his way straight home from school or from work. He was not allowed to see any of his friends in his free time. The only thing he was allowed to do was play football, and he was only allowed to play football if Reverend Benjamin drove him to and from each practice and each match.

'Jerome,' his mum told him, 'the only things that matter are your marks in the classroom, and how well you play every Sunday. And if you do badly at school, then there is no more football for you, and you are not going on social media until your marks improve.'

Jerome didn't argue. He just wanted his mum to be happy with him again, and so he worked harder than ever.

His mum agreed that if he woke up one hour earlier each morning he could go for a run and practise his skills in the park, and after dinner each evening he did an extra hour of reading. Whenever he, his mum and Larry sat down for a meal the atmosphere was serious and quiet, as if they were at a church service.

The only person who was really enjoying himself in the flat was Larry. He had just been given some extra pay, and he couldn't stop telling Jerome about it. 'You see me getting more money?' he asked Jerome. 'That's my reward for hard work. People like you need to know that this doesn't just come easily. When you get to the real world you will see that. Some people think money just comes quick, that you can just walk into other people's houses and take it. No,' he said. 'It's not like that. You need time and patience.'

Jerome looked at him and pretended to listen, and thought to himself: *Yes, Jerome. Time and patience. In less than five years, you will be able to move out.*

But, as Jerome soon found out, it would not take him that long.

Five weeks after Aaron was arrested, Jerome was walking home from school when he got a call from his mum. He put his phone to his ear at once.

'Hi, Mum,' he said, 'don't worry, I'm just on my way home.'

'Oh, don't go home – go back to school,' she replied. 'I'll see you there – we are meeting Mr Morgan in half an hour.'

Oh no, thought Jerome. His throat went dry, and his stomach turned tense. *A meeting with the headmaster?* What had he done now? Had the police found out he was with Aaron that night? He wanted to ask what it was about, but he didn't want to upset his mum any more than he already had. He turned around immediately and began to run in the same direction he had just come.

When Jerome got back to the school building, most of the students had already left. He walked quickly through three empty corridors and up two flights of stairs and then turned right, towards the office of the headmaster, Mr Morgan. It was at the very end of the floor, the very end of the school world. You only went there if you had done something to make the school proud or if you were in trouble. *I can't even make my mum proud*, thought Jerome, *so it can't be that*. He stood outside the bright red door of the office, took a long, slow breath, and knocked twice.

'Come in,' said Mr Morgan. His voice was so low and deep that it rolled under the door, like a wave rushing up the beach and over Jerome's shoes. 'Very good,' he said, as Jerome entered the room. *That doesn't mean anything*, thought Jerome. Mr Morgan always said, 'Very good.' It was just something he said while he was thinking of what he really wanted to say. You could tell Mr Morgan that the sun had fallen out of the sky and had set fire to every tree on earth, and he would just nod and say, 'Very good.'

Mr Morgan was sitting behind his desk, with the palms

of his hands flat on its surface. There were four seats in front of his desk, one of which was empty. In the other seats were Jerome's mum, Ian, and a man he had thought he had seen before but was not sure where.

'Ian!' said Jerome. Ian had a very serious look on his face. He looked at Jerome, smiled quickly, then went back to looking very serious again. 'Mum,' he said. His mum nodded. She was looking nearly as serious as Ian. The man introduced himself.

'Michael Baxter,' he said. 'I always like to meet potential students in person. Please, take a seat.'

Jerome sat down next to him.

'Very good,' said Mr Morgan. He placed his hands together, as if he were about to pray. 'Jerome,' he said, 'I hear it has been a very busy few weeks for you.'

Jerome thought back to that Saturday night when he was running from the police officer.

'Lots of hard work,' he said.

'Very good,' said Mr Morgan. 'Everyone has noticed the effort you are making. Especially Mr Baxter here.'

'Yes,' said Mr Baxter. 'Let me explain. And Jerome – please don't look so afraid.'

'Oh,' said Jerome. He didn't realize but he had been sitting with his shoulders so high that they were almost next to his ears. He relaxed and let them sink.

'Last month,' continued Mr Baxter, 'I received a call from Ian, who I have got to know over the years, and who always keeps an eye out for us. He asked if I could send someone from St Joseph's to look at a certain footballer, a very talented and very charming young man by the name of Jerome Jackson. He was so keen that I thought I would send myself.' He smiled. 'And so I have watched your last four matches for Hackney Stallions.'

'That was you!' said Jerome. Now he knew where he recognized this man from: he had seen him wandering around Hackney Marshes on Sunday, but thought he was just taking a regular walk. This man had been scouting him!

'In those matches,' said Mr Baxter, 'you had a total of eleven goals, seven assists. You are very comfortable dribbling and shooting with your left and right foot. You are very good at heading the ball. You don't lose the ball easily. You love scoring goals, and you love making them for others. You never become negative when your team is losing. You encourage and praise your teammates. My final report gave you ninety-two out of a hundred.'

'That's – that's good?' asked Jerome. It sounded good!

'Very good,' said Mr Morgan. 'Mr Baxter could not wait to meet you.'

'It's excellent,' said Mr Baxter. 'Jerome, have you heard of St Joseph's?'

'I don't think so,' said Jerome.

'You haven't heard of us,' said Mr Baxter, 'but you know our work. Let me know if you have heard of the following footballers. Ready?'

'Yes,' said Jerome, gripping the sides of his chair.

'Wesley Mensah.'

'Yes!' said Jerome. 'Right-back for Ajax Amsterdam.'

'Correct,' said Mr Baxter. 'Ezekiel Baptiste.'

'Defensive midfielder, Borussia Dortmund.'

'Superb! And Marcello Mandolin.'

That one was so obvious that Jerome nearly rolled his eyes.

'Forward. Real Madrid.'

'You got it,' said Mr Baxter. 'All three of these footballers are recent graduates from St Joseph's School, a boarding school in Leyton. We give a first-class education to the leading footballers of the future, and we would like to give that education to you. Starting this summer term.'

Jerome opened his mouth to speak but he couldn't form the right words at first.

'Very good,' said Mr Morgan, and winked. Everyone in the room laughed.

'Oh my goodness,' said Jerome. He put a hand to his forehead. 'Mum, this is happening, isn't it? This is really happening?'

Stephanie's voice was trembling, but her face looked as happy as when she would sit on the park bench with Jerome's dad. 'Yes,' she said. 'Yes.'

'It really is,' said Ian. He was grinning now. 'We had a lovely talk with Mr Morgan here. Your grades are good enough for St Joseph's, and they will look after the fees so your mum will not have to pay. You've done so well, Jerome. This is a good chance for you.'

'Ian,' said Jerome, 'I can't believe it.'

'But you have to believe it,' Ian said. 'This is where it all starts. The next stage of the rest of your life.'

Before Jerome realized what he was doing, he put his hand in the air, and counted to the number fifteen. 'Oops!' he said, pulling his hand down and putting it over his mouth.

'Jerome Jackson,' said Mr Baxter, 'did you just celebrate your place at St Joseph's as if you had scored a goal?'

'Yes,' said Jerome. 'I think I just did!'

'Well,' said Mr Baxter, 'that's the enthusiasm we like to see. We will get all the papers drawn up, and we will see you next term.'

'We will be sorry to lose you,' said Mr Morgan. 'St Joseph's will be lucky to have you.'

'Oh,' said Jerome. He suddenly understood what this meant – that he was about to leave behind everyone that he knew. *Be brave, Jerome*, he thought. *Be brave*.

'You can do this,' said Ian. 'You're going to be brilliant.'

'You are,' said Mr Morgan. 'And I think we need to mark this achievement by getting something to eat. Good news deserves a meal! Any ideas?'

Ian looked at Stephanie and Jerome, then looked back at Mr Morgan.

'There is a great place round the corner,' he said, 'where you can get very good pepper soup.'

PART 2

CROWN

9

TOO FAST

It was Jerome's first week at St Joseph's, and he already wanted to go home. Everything was too big and everything moved too fast.

He knew he was in trouble from the moment he arrived, when Reverend Benjamin drove him through the school gates and through a long valley of tall trees and past the huge emerald fields and up the vast driveway. The main school building was the size of a palace, its stone glowing golden under the afternoon sun. Around him, boys climbed out of cars which cost more than his mum's flat, said goodbye to their parents, then dragged their luggage across the yard. No one noticed Jerome, because they were so busy greeting each other after the holidays, and so for his first few minutes at St Joseph's he just stood there on the tarmac, feeling like a fool in his new uniform as everyone dashed about.

He looked down at his clothes and thought, *This looks ridiculous.* He didn't mind the black trousers and black shoes and white shirt – they were OK – but he didn't like the light brown V-neck pullover, he wasn't keen on the dark green blazer and the dark green tie, and he hated the light brown flat cap. The first time he had seen himself in the mirror, he had thought, *This is horrible; it is so old-fashioned. I look like I belong in a black-and-white photograph.* His mum had been so proud. 'Look at you, Jerome,' she had said, 'a little man!' He didn't feel like a little man, though. He felt like a frightened toddler.

At last he found the courage to ask someone where he was meant to be staying. They showed him to his accommodation, and while he unpacked his things he suddenly felt as if he were about to cry. He had never been away from home like this before. That night he looked out from his bedroom window, trying to see if he could see Hackney, but the trees were so tall that all he could see above them was the stars.

For his first few weeks at school, Jerome was just learning rules, rules and more rules. He had to get up at this time and go to that building for that lesson and talk to that teacher that way and walk on that side of that street. The school had five hundred students, who stayed in ten boarding houses, with fifty boys in each house. Every student had his own bedroom, and in each house there was a lounge where the students could play pool and table tennis against each other and watch television together. There was a main dining room where they all had their meals and a kitchen where they could practise their own cooking. Jerome's house was run by a very tall, very thin man called William Franklin, who was very strict. Whenever he walked into the room everybody sat up or stood up, as if they were trying to show him that they were always ready for hard work.

And the work was hard. It was so, so hard. The tests were so difficult that Jerome came out of each class thinking that his brain was half the size of everybody else's. Most of these boys spoke three languages and played one instrument. Most of the boys here had lots of money, too. They had fancy voices, like the prime minister. Their parents were bankers or lawyers or doctors or business owners or footballers. They went on holiday to small islands that Jerome had never heard of, and some of them showed Jerome pictures of their houses, which were bigger than St Joseph's School. Jerome never showed them pictures of his flat, because he was embarrassed by how small it was.

But he still couldn't wait to play football against his fellow students for the first time. *I'll show them why I'm here*, he thought. *I belong at this school just as much as any of them.* It took a week for Jerome to have his first training session, and by then everyone was excited to see him play. Everyone had heard about this amazing footballer from East London who had been recommended by Ian

Wright, and now they were curious to see what the fuss was about. They had so many questions for him, such as:

'What kind of tricks can you do?'

'How many times can you keep the ball up?'

'Which big clubs are interested in you?'

'Are you going to win the UK Schools Cup for us this year?'

And so on. Jerome didn't talk very much at first, because he didn't have a fancy voice like many of the other students. He just kept repeating the same thing: 'When you watch me play football, then you'll see.'

***

On Friday afternoon Jerome jogged down for his first football training session, which was in full view of the school's main building. He got there twenty minutes early, to impress Mr Baxter. But one boy was already there, with his back to Jerome, shooting at an empty net. He seemed not to notice as Jerome approached, but all of a sudden, he turned and thrashed a ball towards Jerome without warning. The ball came so fast that before Jerome could raise his foot to stop it, it had already bounced off his shins. The boy watched the ball roll away to a halt, then smiled.

'You must be Ian Wright's boy,' he said.

'I'm not anyone's boy,' said Jerome.

'I'm Gavin,' said the boy. 'I'm the best striker here, and the team captain.'

'But Mr Baxter hasn't chosen the team captain for this year yet,' said Jerome.

'When he does,' said Gavin, 'it will be me.' He turned back to face the goal, and Jerome walked over to the ball that had hit him. He looked at Gavin, then stabbed his foot underneath the ball, so quickly that it floated straight up from the earth, drifting forward as slowly as a cloud of smoke, before bouncing off the top of Gavin's head. Gavin turned around, his cheeks darkening with rage.

'That was dangerous,' he said.

'No,' said Jerome, 'it was on target.'

The two of them stared at each other for a few seconds, and then other students started to arrive at the training ground.

'Hey, Gavin! Gavin, knock it over here!'

Gavin shook his head and hit a long pass towards the boy who had called for it.

'See you in a real game,' he said, pointing to the pitch. 'Then we will see who can play.'

By the time everyone had turned up to the training session, there were twenty-four boys, and they did a series of exercises: first some sprints, then some passes, then some shooting. This was where Jerome had his first shock. When he played in Hackney, he was easily the quickest player in any game. Here, he was still the quickest – but not by much. During a passing exercise, where three players stood in a circle around Jerome and passed the ball to each other while he tried to tackle them, he chased and chased and chased them, but he didn't get the ball once — they were just too good. When he came to do shooting practice, he was already so exhausted that he had to lie flat out on the grass to recover, breathing hard. When he stood up to shoot towards goal, his eyes widened. There, standing in front of him twenty yards away, was the largest thirteen-year-old he had ever seen. Billy Seymour was already over six feet tall and had hands the size of dinner plates.

'Ah,' said Jerome.

'Let's see what you do against that,' came Gavin's voice from behind him.

Jerome ran up to the ball and struck it hard. It sailed towards goal, on its way into the top corner of the net — and Billy, who seemed almost bored, looked across at it, stuck out his left hand, and caught it.

'Oh my God,' said Jerome, as the players behind him gasped. Among them, he heard Gavin laughing.

'Welcome to St Joe's,' said Gavin.

Jerome hit some better shots after that, but he still didn't manage to score past Billy for the rest of the session. Gavin, meanwhile, scored with ease. There were two times when he shot with so much force that Billy didn't even move as the ball entered the net.

At the end of the training session, Mr Baxter divided them into two teams.

'Jerome,' said Mr Baxter, 'I know you like playing as

the central striker, but today I'm putting you on the left wing. Just to see what you can do out there. OK?'

'OK,' said Jerome. He looked ahead of him and nodded. He was ready!

'You're not going to enjoy this,' said Gavin, as he walked to his half of the pitch.

The first time Jerome got the ball and dribbled at Toby, he was surprised to hear Toby shout, 'He's going left.' Toby stuck out his leg, touched the ball away from Jerome, and passed it to a teammate. The next time Jerome ran at Toby, the same thing happened.

'He's going right,' called Toby, and looked at his teammate. 'Got him.'

Oh no, thought Jerome. *He always knows exactly what I'm going to do.* This was like being in a computer game where the opponents were a level smarter than him.

By now, all the other boys were finishing their training sessions, and they were walking past the pitch where Jerome was playing. Many of them stopped to watch the new boy. All they saw was a footballer who kept getting the ball, running ten yards with it, and then losing it – again, and again, and again. They lost interest and walked away, and soon almost no one was watching any more. When the whistle finally went for the end of the match, Jerome was so ashamed. All he wanted to do was go home and lie in bed and pull the sheets over his head, and never leave his bedroom until everyone forgot about him.

As he shook hands with the players on the other team to thank them for the game, he saw Mr Baxter walking over to him.

'Jerome,' he said, 'don't worry about today. Everyone has a tough first few practices at St Joe's. You'll get there.' But that didn't make Jerome feel any better. Maybe his dream was going to be even harder work than he thought.

10

THIS IS THE LIFE

Three days after Jerome's first training session, St Joseph's football coaches announced who was in the Junior Firsts squad for the first game of the season. The list was posted on the largest message board in the main school building, and dozens of schoolboys rushed to it after breakfast to see who had been selected. Jerome didn't rush, though. He knew he hadn't been chosen to start for the first eleven – not after playing like that. When much of the crowd had moved away, he stepped forward and looked at the team for himself. The captain was Gavin Bradley. Toby Saltman in defence. Kieran Frame and Eugene Davis in midfield, that made sense. Of course Billy Seymour was in goal. And then he saw what he had feared. There he was, Jerome Jackson, at the very foot of the page, listed as the last substitute.

Even though Jerome expected bad news, he was still devastated. He stood there in front of the message board, his head slumped forward and his hands on his hips, as if he had just missed a penalty to lose his team the cup final.

'Hey, Jerome. Cheer up, mate.'

Jerome turned around. It was Toby, the same boy who had made his first training session such hell, who would be starting in the first eleven while Jerome was on the bench.

'That's easy for you to say,' he replied.

'Yes, maybe it is,' said Toby. 'But Jerome, you can't expect everything to be perfect at once. You've only been at St Joseph's for five minutes. I bet you don't even know where the fives courts are.'

'The what?' asked Jerome.

'Exactly,' said Toby. 'You're still settling in. New school, new subjects, everything. So don't be too hard on yourself. It's obvious that you are a great footballer. You'll prove that.'

'If I'm such a great footballer,' said Jerome, 'then why was it so easy for you to stop me every single time?'

'Because you are showing me what you are doing,' said Toby. He pointed to the ground just in front of Jerome's feet. 'Look down here,' he said. 'Each time you were running towards me, I watched the foot that you weren't kicking the ball with. That foot always points in the direction where you are about to move. You just need to hide that. And you can do that; you're good enough.'

Jerome thought for a moment. 'Why are you telling me this? You're my competition; you shouldn't be helping me.'

'Because you've got guts,' said Toby. 'Every time I tackled you, you kept coming back; you kept trying. Most forwards lose confidence, but you didn't. Even when everyone was watching you.'

'It didn't get me anywhere though,' said Jerome. 'I'm on the bench, like a loser.'

'Jerome.' Toby sounded stern now. 'Look at all the names in that squad. There's only one of them who Ian Wright looked at and begged this school to take. And that is you.' He prodded his finger in the middle of Jerome's chest. 'You,' he said, and prodded again. 'You,' he said, and prodded again. 'You.'

Jerome laughed, stepping back. 'You weirdo!' he said. 'Get away from me!' He wiped a tear from the corner of his eye, but he was crying from happiness. 'Toby, you are so odd.'

'You've got that right,' Toby said, with a grin. 'Now that you understand me, let's go for a walk. You need to know your way around here.'

They strolled away from the main school building, across the lawn, and past the theatre, where some of the students would put on plays and concerts. 'That over there,' said Toby, 'those are the fives courts. It's like playing squash, only you play it with padded gloves instead of a squash racket. Weird game. But a lot of fun once you get to know it.'

They walked on to the gardens, which had a large marble fountain at their centre. On the side of the fountain was a list of names. 'Now look at this,' said Toby, and pointed to the bottom of the list. 'What does that say?'

'This monument,' read Jerome, 'was built thanks to the generosity of the Bradley family.'

'Right,' said Toby. 'That's why Gavin Bradley walks around like he owns the place. Because, in a way, his family *does* own the place. Gavin is so confident because everyone has always told him that he is the best. Imagine how good you will be when *you* start telling yourself you are the best.' They carried on walking and, for the first time since Jerome arrived at St Joseph's, his shoulders felt less heavy.

'Can I ask you something?' asked Toby, after a short while. He suddenly sounded a little anxious.

'Sure,' said Jerome.

Toby took a breath.

'I'm a massive Arsenal fan so I wanted to know what Ian Wright was actually like?'

'Ha! Oh, that,' said Jerome.

'I mean,' said Toby, 'I don't want you thinking I'm being nice to you just because you know someone famous.'

'Toby,' said Jerome, 'if you were trying to be nice to me, you wouldn't have embarrassed me in front of everyone at training.'

'Good point,' said Toby, laughing.

'It's funny with Ian,' said Jerome. 'I haven't known him for long, but it feels like I've known him for ages. You know how in your family you always have a favourite uncle? Well, Ian is like that.'

'Ah, so he's actually a mate of yours?'

Jerome shrugged. 'I guess so, yeah.'

'Wow,' said Toby. 'My granddad is going to love that. He used to go to Highbury every week to see Ian play.'

'Who knows,' said Jerome, 'he might even come down and watch me play one day.'

'You'd better improve before then,' said Toby, and then a wicked smile rolled across his face. 'You don't want to look silly in front of your uncle.'

'Oi!' Jerome aimed a slap at Toby, but Toby was already out of reach, and running away across the yard.

'I knew you were going to try and slap me,' he yelled back at Jerome, laughing. 'I always know what you are going to do. Stop showing me!'

That weekend St Joseph's played their first game of the season, at home against Stafford College. Jerome's mum couldn't come to see him play because she had extra shifts at work, but he told her not to worry.

I'm only on the bench, Mum. I'll only play for a couple of minutes

I still wish I could
be there. Ian will
be so happy they
have picked you for
the first team, I'll
let him know

Thanks so much, Mum

I asked Larry if
he would come and
support you, but he
said that schoolboys'
football wasn't
really his thing

It's OK, Mum

He says he prefers
watching adults, it's
nothing personal

He wanted to write, *with Larry it's always something personal*, but he didn't.

It's OK

How is school?

The classes are hard but the teachers are nice. They are really trying to help me. Geography is OK. And English. Physics is difficult but chemistry is fun. And I'm making a couple of friends.

Can't wait to hear all about it when you get home

Can't wait to tell you! Love you Mum

Love you too

***

The good thing about football was that wherever Jerome played, the feeling was always the same in the dressing room before the match: the nerves and the quiet excitement, the smell of the muscle spray, the scratch of the chalk on the tactics board. *This is home*, he thought, as he took his kit from the bag: dark green shirt with the number 15 on the back, gold shorts, dark green socks.

He didn't like the school colours at first, but now he was getting used to them – they made him feel different, and special. When they walked out on to the pitch, there were hundreds of boys and parents ready to watch them, and even a few girls from Queen Elizabeth's, the nearby girls' boarding school. Even though he wasn't in the starting eleven, Jerome felt a rush of pride in his stomach. It was the biggest crowd he had ever seen. *This is the life*, he thought. *I could get used to this.*

When the game started, Jerome couldn't believe how quick it was. Stafford's players were a little bigger than St Joseph's, but St Joseph's were faster and more skilful. The game was mostly St Joseph's defending for a long time, then rushing forward to attack. Gavin Bradley scored the first goal after fifteen minutes, a swirling free kick from twenty yards into the bottom corner, and ten minutes from the end of the game he scored the second, running through after a pass from their quietly excellent left back, Tim Thorogood. When he scored that final goal, he ran towards the crowd, and dozens of students leapt on him as he celebrated. Jerome watched from the touchline and cheered, and as Gavin ran past, he even thought he saw Gavin smile at him.

In the dressing room afterwards, Jerome sat there until everyone else had left. He didn't know how to feel: he was happy that his team had won, but sad that he didn't get a chance to play. Mr Baxter saw him sitting there and walked over to him.

'Any space for me on that bench, Jerome?' he asked.

'Sure thing, sir,' he said, and Mr Baxter took a seat next to him.

'I know we didn't use you today, Jerome,' said Mr Baxter. 'We are easing you in, getting you used to the pace of the game. But your time will come, it really will.'

'I know,' said Jerome.

'You don't sound like you believe it,' said Mr Baxter. His voice was gentle, as if he were asking a question.

'I don't right now,' said Jerome. He thought about Aaron sitting in a locked room, his life changed for ever. He thought about Larry spitting on the carpet. He thought about his mum so tired and so busy that she could never afford a holiday. He thought of his school, and of all the people he left behind for this alien place.

'Do you know what Ian told me about you?' asked Mr Baxter. 'That first time he called me, do you know what he said?'

Jerome looked at him and shook his head.

'He said: this boy Jerome is something special. It's not the skill, he's got loads of that. Or the speed. Or even what he sees on the pitch. It's like – the more you heat the situation up, the calmer he gets. Not everyone responds to heat like that. As a professional footballer, you don't just have to like fire. You have to love it.'

'Yes,' said Jerome, at once. 'I do love it.'

'Spoken like a true professional.' Mr Baxter smiled. 'We will drop you in the fire soon, Jerome.'

'I'm ready, always,' said Jerome.

'That's the spirit,' said Mr Baxter. 'Now, let's get out of here. There's food and drink at the cricket pavilion, and we have a win to celebrate.'

11

UNPREDICTABLE

Jerome was going home to Hackney for half-term, and that Friday afternoon he had a choice. Either he could go home in the clothes he normally wore, a hoodie and tracksuit bottoms, or he could go home wearing his St Joseph's school uniform. He still felt embarrassed by his uniform, and he knew that the only way he would stop feeling like that was to wear it until the shame went away. He decided to be brave. He packed some clothes in his rucksack, put on his blazer and his flat cap, and off he went.

The journey from Leytonstone to Hackney was only forty-five minutes: he had to walk to the Underground station, then change at Stratford, then get the Overground train. When he first got on the train, he was frightened to make eye contact with anyone, but then he realized that no one else really noticed or even cared what he was wearing. He saw his reflection in the glass of the train's window and thought, *I should feel proud, these clothes are so smart.* By the time he got to Hackney, he was hoping that he would see people he knew, so that he could show off his new look.

He got his wish. As he walked down the steps of Hackney Central train station, he bumped into Ikenna, from the Hackney Methodist football team. As soon as Ikenna saw him, his face unfolded into a huge smile.

'Damn, Jerome!' said Ikenna. 'Nice garms. Wait till the girls see you in those!'

'I don't care about that stuff,' said Jerome.

Ikenna rolled his eyes. 'Everyone cares about that stuff,' he replied.

Jerome did care. In fact, he was hoping he would see Michelle in the street, but he didn't. He hadn't seen or heard from her since Aaron and Amira got arrested. But he did see a couple of boys from his old school, who had been a few years above him: they looked him up and down, and they nodded. *Good for you,* their faces said. By the time Jerome walked back into his estate, he was feeling so happy that he could have floated out of his shoes. At the foot of his stairwell, he heard a familiar voice.

'Look at you, Little Tin!' called Mrs Malone, looking down from her balcony. 'You are looking like a gentleman and a scholar.'

'Thanks very much, Mrs Malone!' said Jerome.

'And that hat, too – very stylish! You look like somebody off the television. Like a celebrity.'

Now Jerome *was* embarrassed about his uniform, but in a good way. He climbed the steps to his flat, and was going to get out his key, but the front door was already open. Larry was standing there, as if he could sense Jerome's arrival.

'Well, well,' he said. 'You've been gone a couple of weeks and suddenly you are walking around like the King of Hackney.'

Jerome was trying to smile, just to be nice, but then he understood too late that this was a bad idea.

'You think that's funny, do you?' Larry thrust his face so close to Jerome's that Jerome could smell the grease from Larry's lunch on his breath, and he stopped smiling.

'No,' said Jerome. 'I was just trying to greet you.'

'Very interesting,' said Larry. 'You've got a bit more aggressive already.' He kept his face close to Jerome's but the boy didn't blink. 'It only took you a few weeks,' said Larry. 'Hanging out with those lords and ladies and you already think you're better than people. You think you're better than me, don't you?'

Jerome blinked.

'There he is,' said Larry. 'Same old Jerome. There he is.' Happy that he had intimidated him, Larry stepped back. As he did so, he looked to his left, and he saw Mrs Malone standing a few metres away. She was watching him sternly, her eyes cold as a winter morning.

'Don't you dare speak to Jerome like that,' she said. 'His own father would not have spoken to him like that, so what gives you the right?' She nodded at Jerome. 'You go inside now,' she said, and Jerome gratefully did so. 'You leave him alone,' she continued.

'Yes – yes,' said Larry, confused by this small woman who was speaking to him like she was his army officer. Jerome tried to listen to their conversation from his bedroom but couldn't quite hear them. But whatever Mrs Malone said to Larry must have worked, because Larry came into the flat ten minutes later and didn't say anything to Jerome. He just walked into the living room, closed the door, and sat in there until the evening when Jerome's mum got home.

A couple of days later Jerome went to Uncle Ray's, to see Ian for the first time since he started at St Joseph's. When he walked in, he noticed that it was a little busier than usual, with a couple of young children running round one of the empty chairs, and Uncle Ray arguing loudly with a customer about who Arsenal should buy in the summer. Ian was behind the decks, and he looked up and took off his headphones as Jerome walked in.

'My man!' he exclaimed, walking to the front of the shop to embrace Jerome. 'How is St Joseph's?'

'It's amazing,' said Jerome. 'And a bit overwhelming, to be honest. I'm still getting used to it.' He pointed to the speakers. 'What's this old stuff?'

'This old stuff is the great Jean Carn,' said Ian. 'The

track is called "Don't Let It Go To Your Head".'

'It's quite good,' said Jerome.

'Quite good!' said Ian. 'When you listen to such tunes you are listening to greatness!'

'Hey, Jerome! I'll be with you in a moment,' said Uncle Ray. 'I'm just trying to educate this fellow here about Arsenal.'

'Educate me!' said the man.

'Young man, I was watching Arsenal when your parents were flirting at the local pub,' said Uncle Ray.

'True. You were watching Arsenal before they invented the wheel,' said the young man, and Uncle Ray laughed so hard he dropped his pot of shaving cream.

'Leonie,' said Uncle Ray, calling one of the young children. He wiped his eyes. 'Please get some paper towel for your grandpa – he's made a mess.'

'Yes, Granddad!' shouted Leonie, and disappeared.

'Family visit today,' explained Ian, turning back to Jerome. 'So,' he said, sitting in a nearby seat. 'What's new? I want to hear it all.'

'It's Larry,' said Jerome. 'He's kind of got worse since I started boarding school.'

'Worse?' asked Ian. 'But you don't see him.'

'I think that's it,' said Jerome. 'I cooked for him and Mum last night and it just made him more angry. I think when I was gone, he was happy, because he had Mum all to himself. And now I'm back and I think he is jealous.'

Ian nodded. 'You know what else it is, Jerome,' he said.

'He's angry because now you are at that school, he is scared you are going to escape.'

'But he always makes me feel like I'm in the way,' said Jerome.

'I know,' said Ian. 'But I've been around situations like that. And people like that always change the rules. You can never make them happy. They hate having you in the flat, so they bully you. But if you leave the flat, they get more angry, because they know one day they won't be able to bully you any more. You can't win.'

'Then what do I do?' asked Jerome.

'You just keep focusing on your work and your football,' said Ian. 'That's the only way. How's that really going, by the way?'

'School's fine,' said Jerome. 'I mean, it's not fine, I'm bottom of most classes. But they say that's normal at this stage.' He hesitated. 'But my football is not going so well. I thought I was better than this.' He told Ian all about the very difficult training sessions. He talked about how there was a boy called Toby, a very good defender and a big Arsenal fan who made him look silly, but then they became friends and now Toby was helping him settle in. He told Ian about how Gavin Bradley was being mean to him. The more he spoke, the more Ian smiled. By the time he finished talking, Ian was leaning back in his chair with both his hands behind his head and with his eyes shut, as if he were sunbathing. 'Ian?' asked Jerome nervously. *Oh no*, he thought, *I hope he hasn't fallen asleep.*

But Ian was wide awake. He was just making a plan.

'Jerome,' he said. 'You're lucky. Because you have had a tough start, you now have the perfect chance to surprise everyone.'

'What do you mean?'

'That first time I saw you play, I saw it. One of the greatest skills you have is that you are unpredictable. You have the ability to make chances from anywhere.' Ian opened his eyes and sat forward. 'Here's what you do from now on, in training and in matches. You normally use your right foot, don't you? To control the ball, and to shoot it.'

Jerome nodded.

'From now on,' said Ian, 'don't do that. Start using your left foot much more. Don't make a big fuss about it. Just turn up at training next week and use your left foot whenever you can. Defenders will start expecting it. They will start to mark you differently. And then, just when they are used to it, change back to your right foot again. That will make them anxious. Suddenly they won't know what to do with you. They will stop standing so close to you because they won't know which way you will turn.'

'Wow. I feel like I should be writing this down,' said Jerome.

'It's OK,' said Ian. 'You're smart, you'll remember. And when they stop standing so close to you, they will give you room to shoot. And we both know you can shoot.'

'Yes, I definitely can,' said Jerome.

'Good man,' said Ian. 'So next time you play, you need to shoot within two minutes of getting on the pitch. I don't care how far from goal you are. Your job is to make every team scared of you the second you cross the halfway line. They need to see your confidence.'

Jerome fidgeted nervously. 'I don't feel very confident though,' he said.

'Nonsense!' said Ian. 'What's your full name?'

'Jerome Jackson?' said Jerome.

'Louder!' cried Ian, as if he was leading a church service on a Sunday.

'Jerome Jackson,' said Jerome awkwardly.

'Louder!' repeated Ian, raising his hands above his head. He turned to Uncle Ray and his grandchildren and his customer. 'Say it with me, Uncle Ray's!'

'Jerome Jackson!' they yelled, as loud as they could. 'JEROME JACKSON!'

'You people are ridiculous,' said Jerome, laughing.

'Just telling you the facts,' said Ian. 'Every time you go out to play, you need to have those cheers in your head. You are box office, Jerome. One day we will all be paying a lot of money to see you. Never forget that.' He made Jerome take his hand. 'Promise,' he said.

'Promise,' said Jerome, and they shook on it.

'That's what I like to hear,' said Ian. 'Now let's play

some tunes, while Ray sorts out the top of your head. We need to get you looking fresh for your comeback.' He passed Jerome an apron, in preparation for his haircut. 'Oh – and your mate Toby. I need to do a video for him!'

'Really?' said Jerome.

'Of course! He's been helping you out, right?'

'Well, yes, but—'

'Then we've got to sort him out. You've always got to sort your mates out,' said Ian. 'Here, give me your phone.' Jerome handed his phone to Ian, who selected the video app, smiled into the screen, then started to film himself.

'Hi, Toby,' he said, then stopped. 'Jerome, what's his full name?'

'Toby Saltman.'

'Mr Toby Saltman,' continued Ian, 'it's Wrighty here, broadcasting from Uncle Ray's, the finest barbershop in Britain. My young associate here' – he pointed at Jerome – 'tells me that you are a supporter of Arsenal FC, which is, of course, by far the greatest team the world has ever seen. I would like to thank you, first of all, for loving Arsenal. I would also like to thank you for being so kind to Jerome in his first few weeks at St Joseph's. And when I come to watch Jerome one day, let's hang out.' He handed back the phone to Jerome, who was beaming.

'Oh wow,' said Jerome. 'He is going to love this so

much!' He sent the video to Toby, and a few minutes later he heard a zing as Toby replied with a video of his own. He pressed play, and all everyone in the barbershop heard was:

'Oh my God ... Ian Wright! Oh my God ... Oh my God, oh my God!'

'You think he liked it?' said Ian and winked. 'Always got to help your friends out!'

12

A FOOTBALL GENIUS

It was the first training session after half-term for St Joseph's Junior Firsts, and Jerome was there before anyone else. He was there so early that, by the time Gavin Bradley arrived, he had already laid out all the cones and taken out all the footballs.

'You won't get into the starting eleven by sucking up,' said Gavin.

'Oh, I know that,' said Jerome. 'Hope you had a nice half-term break, by the way.'

'Ah,' said Gavin. He was not expecting such a friendly answer. 'I did actually.'

'Where did you go?'

'Cornwall. My family has a house there.'

Your family probably has a house everywhere, thought Jerome. 'That sounds great,' he replied.

'Have you ever been to Cornwall?'

'A long time ago,' said Jerome. 'We went to a place called Tencreek, I think. We stayed in a caravan.'

Gavin smiled. 'I know that place very well,' he said.

'Oh really?' said Jerome.

'Yes,' said Gavin. 'That's a place you stay when you haven't got lots of money.'

'Oh,' said Jerome. Then he said, 'Well, we don't have lots of money, so that makes sense.'

'I suppose it does,' Gavin said.

'I had a holiday where I did lots of stuff that you can't buy,' said Jerome.

'You can buy anything if you have enough money,' said Gavin.

'No, you can't,' said Jerome. 'There are some people who won't be your friend even if you give them a million pounds.'

'Rubbish,' Gavin replied, but he looked nervous when he heard that. He tried another attack.

'You'd better be good in training today,' he said. 'People are saying you are overhyped.'

'Interesting,' said Jerome. 'Let's see what people say tonight.'

He smiled, and Gavin looked nervous again.

The training session went quickly. Jerome had been working hard on his fitness, so he was even faster now, and when he passed the ball, he was more relaxed, more patient. When it came to the shooting exercises, he hit the ball with greater power, and with more swerve. He scored past Billy three times out of five, and one of the goals was so good that Billy nodded at him as he threw the ball back.

As always, to end the session, the boys played a game of eleven-a-side. That went even better for Jerome. He was against Toby again, out on the left wing, and after two minutes the ball came to him, a pass hit hard along the ground from the left touchline. Toby rushed forward, ready to make the tackle. Jerome ran towards the ball as fast he could, and then, just before Toby got there, he stopped, put his foot under the ball and flicked it one metre in the air.

Toby swung his leg where he thought the ball would be but missed it completely; he skidded past Jerome on his bottom, like a child going down a waterslide. Jerome pushed the ball onwards with his right foot and started sprinting towards goal. The other defenders looked on in shock. They had expected Toby to make that tackle and now they couldn't get to that side of the area in time. Jerome was alone, ten yards from the penalty area, and it was just him against Billy.

Billy advanced a few yards, preparing for Jerome to slow down and shoot, because he knew that when Jerome was a long way from goal he only liked to shoot with his right foot. That's why he was still getting ready to put his arms up when he saw Jerome strike the ball with his left foot, and that's why he didn't even have time to jump before the ball, flying high and swift as a hawk, tore through the air and over his head and into the far corner of his net.

'Jerome, you beauty!' Jerome looked round to see Toby, still on the floor where Jerome had left him, clenching his fists with joy, his voice full of pride. 'There he is,' Toby continued, pointing to Jerome. 'I told you! A football genius!'

Jerome wished he could have had a video camera to record the next few seconds for ever. There was Billy Seymour, his hands helpless by his side. There were the rest of his teammates, a bewildered look across each of their faces, because nobody, nobody ever did that to Billy. There was Mr Baxter, his arms folded, trying not to show how delighted he was. And, finally, there was Gavin, standing twenty yards away, looking at Jerome with a glare that could have pierced steel. On his way back to the halfway line for kick-off, Jerome made sure that he jogged past Gavin, so that Gavin was close enough to hear him whisper one question:

'So, Gavin, am I overhyped?'

***

That goal changed Jerome's entire term. Now he felt as if he belonged at St Joseph's, and he was so much more confident in class too. The more he believed in himself, the better his marks got. He was one of the best at English and for history he got the top grade in his class for his essay about the Tudors. In his chemistry class, where he normally finished close to the bottom, he even got the fourth-best mark in a test out of twenty students. He was really enjoying his life in the house too. When he wasn't working or playing sport, he kept practising his cooking in the house kitchen, and he was getting really good at it. One day he made a stew so good that Darius Vernon, one of the boys in his house, suggested that he should start selling it.

'Honestly,' said Darius, 'this stuff could make you a fortune.'

'You're a joker,' said Jerome. 'It's nothing special.'

'Seriously,' said Darius. 'I've seen it. These boarding school kids love Jamaican food. They like a taste of exotic things.'

'Exotic!' Jerome rolled his eyes. 'Darius, I'm from Hackney.'

'For a lot of these boys Hackney *is* exotic,' said Darius. 'Look. Let's do a business plan. You cook the food; I brand it and I sell it. We sort out delivery to different houses. We split the profits.' Darius shrugged. 'Easy.'

'Darius,' said Jerome, 'it's not that easy.'

Darius was always looking for ways to make money – he got that from his dad, who owned hundreds of companies and was always setting up new ones. The companies were all in countries far away, like Anguilla and Aruba and Bermuda and Belize. 'First thing – I don't have the kind of money to buy food to cook for that many people.'

'Then I'll be your first investor!' said Darius.

'Second thing,' said Jerome, 'it's against the school rules. It's illegal to trade goods on school grounds and in the surrounding area.'

Darius sighed. 'Jerome, you will never make any money if you always play by the rules,' he said.

Jerome thought about Aaron. 'Maybe not,' he said, 'but I definitely won't go to prison.'

Darius laughed. 'Prison! Jerome, you are so dramatic. No one goes to prison,' he replied, and then he helped himself to more stew.

That next Saturday, as Jerome warmed up before the Junior Firsts' game against Isambard School, he noticed that some things were different about the watching crowd. There were many more of them this time – at the start of the season, there were maybe seventy people watching them, but now there were more than two hundred. There were lots of girls, too – they must have come from Queen Elizabeth's, because some of them were talking to Gavin Bradley, and Gavin knew everyone. And there were several people he hadn't seen before – some of them were wearing tracksuits, some of them were wearing blazers and smart trousers, but they definitely weren't teachers. Toby saw Jerome looking at the touchline and came over to explain.

'Those men over there,' he said, 'are football

scouts. Don't look now,' he said quickly. 'They come a few times each year, just to check in on us. That one's from Southampton' – he leaned his head slightly in the direction of each man – 'he's from Liverpool, she's from Borussia Dortmund, and the last one in the black tracksuit is from Atalanta.'

'I bet most of them are here for Gavin Bradley,' said Jerome.

'Don't be so sure,' said Toby. 'The scouts are a funny lot. It's hard to know what they're looking for. The other time they came here everyone thought they were watching Danny Maxwell, and they ended up signing Ezekiel Baptiste.'

'But Ezekiel Baptiste must have been the man when he was here,' said Jerome. 'He's big!'

'He's big now,' said Toby. 'But football is strange like that. The ones who make it aren't always the ones you think.'

'Do you want to make it, Toby? You never talk about it.'

'Who, me?' asked Toby. 'I don't know, to be honest. I know I'm good enough. It just feels like too much risk – to put everything to one side to be a footballer. If you want to make it as a footballer, I feel like it has to be your only dream. And I don't want it to be my only dream.'

'But lots of footballers do other things with their lives,' said Jerome. 'Some of them have charities and businesses and things.'

'Yes,' said Toby, 'but they have to be desperate to make

it, you know? And I don't think I'm *desperate*.'

'I know,' said Jerome. 'I'm desperate.'

'You there!' called Mr Baxter. 'Toby and Jerome! You're gossiping like two old men at the market. Make sure you concentrate. We will need big games from you today.' He jogged over towards them. 'Toby, if I could just have a minute with Jerome, please.' Toby nodded, and walked towards the centre circle, to join the other players.

'Jerome,' said Mr Baxter, 'I've got a special job for you today. You're starting on the bench, but against this team you are actually our most dangerous player. Does that make sense?'

'Well,' said Jerome, 'not really, sir.'

'The style that Isambard play is very quick, very intense,' said Mr Baxter, 'and it is also exhausting. Their wing-backs do so much work that with about fifteen minutes to go, they're very tired. That's when we are going to bring you on. I want you to attack the spaces that they leave behind when they are tired. With your speed and skill against them, they don't have a chance.'

'Got it,' said Jerome.

'Great,' said Mr Baxter. 'Jerome, your mission when you come on that pitch is to be man of the match. You will only have fifteen minutes to do it, but I know you can. Understood?'

'Understood, sir!' Jerome glanced across at the touchline, so swiftly that the scouts couldn't see him.

'Let's do this!'

And so, with fifteen minutes of the game to go, Jerome's moment came. It had been a great match, but the score was 0–0, and both teams were starting to look tired. Mr Baxter turned to Jerome and nodded, and he took off his tracksuit, ready to step on to the pitch. As he prepared to join the game, he was stunned to see Gavin Bradley walking towards him. Even the home crowd, which was howling its support, went a little quiet.

'Mr Baxter,' said Jerome, 'you're taking Gavin off for me?'

'I believe in you, Jerome,' said Mr Baxter. 'Now get out there and prove me right.'

'Yes, sir,' said Jerome. As Gavin came off the pitch, he put his hands out to give him a high-five, but Gavin didn't even look at him. He took a water bottle from the side of the pitch, laid on his back and closed his eyes.

Jerome didn't care, though. He had a job to do. He started running from the left side to the right side of the pitch and back again.

'Which one of you is marking number 15?' asked one of Isambard's midfielders.

'Not me,' replied one of their defenders, 'he's on the left wing.'

'But he keeps moving,' said another one.

'Then follow him!' said the midfielder.

'He's too quick for that,' said the first defender.

Jerome smiled to himself. *They're already scared*, he thought. *Time to scare them even more*. He got the ball on the left side of the field, right next to the last defender. Instead of running down the wing as would be expected, Jerome turned right and ran straight across the pitch. The opposition were confused. What was he doing? One by one, they started to follow him, but they were not quick enough to keep up – and then, with his head down, at full speed, Jerome backheeled the ball towards Isambard's goal.

As he kept running, he heard the crowd gasp, and he knew that his plan had worked. He had passed the ball into the empty space that everyone had left by chasing him, and now Kieran, who had been waiting for this chance, ran on to Jerome's pass, went round the goalkeeper, and drove the ball into the net. 1–0!

The yell from the crowd was louder than an avalanche, as students and parents hugged each other in celebration and danced down the touchline.

Kieran ran back towards Jerome, pointing at him all the way. 'Yes, Jerome!' he screamed. 'You beauty!'

'Excellent, now get back and defend!' shouted Mr Baxter. 'Concentrate! Focus, St Joseph's, focus!'

Isambard attacked as well as they could, but they just had no more energy, and a few minutes later the referee blew his whistle. St Joseph's had won! Jerome's teammates surrounded him, everyone except Gavin, who had his hands in the pockets of his jacket and was sulking at the back of the joyous crowd. And then the chant started.

Jay-Jay! Jay-Jay! Jay-Jay!

Toby turned to Jerome and winked. 'Fan favourite already, I see?'

'Let's hear it for Jay-Jay!' The whole team walked towards the touchline, with Jerome slightly ahead of them. 'Good work, Jerome,' said Mr Baxter, patting him on the back. The joyous crowd surrounded them, and all Jerome could hear was that glorious chant:

Jay-Jay! Jay-Jay! Jay-Jay! Jay-Jay!

13

JAY-JAY

It wasn't until two weeks later, when Jerome was in a local shop on a Sunday afternoon, that he understood just how far his name was spreading. He was standing in the queue with his schoolfriend Darius, about to pay for a pack of biscuits, when he heard a girl behind them ask: 'Is that Jay-Jay?'

He turned around. There were two girls, about five metres behind them, looking down at one of their phones and then looking up at him.

'Told you!' said one of them and walked towards him.

'Lisa, you are so embarrassing,' said the other girl, who stayed back.

'Yeah,' he said, 'that's me. I play football at St Joseph's.'

'Me and Jessica were watching your goal,' said Lisa.

'The one you scored against Hawkwell.' She showed Jerome and Darius her phone. There, on her screen, was a thirty-second video of his goal from the previous week. The video showed Jerome running towards the edge of Hawkwell's penalty area, the ball flying towards Jerome's waist, and then Jerome jumping off the ground to hit it. He smashed the ball so hard with his left foot that the ball flew into the top-left corner of the net before the goalkeeper could even move. As Jerome's team screamed in celebration, Hawkwell's goalkeeper just stood there blinking sadly, like a cat who had been locked outside in the rain.

'Someone at your school uploaded it to Instagram,' said Jessica. 'We were trying to copy it at training.'

'Wow,' said Darius. 'This video has eighty thousand views! Jerome, you are getting famous!'

'I'm not famous,' Jerome said, but he was enjoying this now. What if he *was* famous?

'Someone even started an account of your skills and goals,' said Lisa. 'It's called jayjayfifteen.' She showed him again. 'It's already got three videos up there.'

'Oh my gosh,' said Darius. 'Jay-Jay Fifteen. What a great name for a brand. We need to turn this into a business!'

'Who are you?' asked Lisa, smiling. 'His agent?'

'Yes, absolutely.' Darius scowled and stood in front of Jerome, as if Jerome were a building and he was a security guard.

'He's being silly,' said Jerome. 'Darius, you are being silly.'

'Maybe he is,' said Lisa. 'But only a little. We saw you playing against Isambard – you were really good. Her brother –' she pointed at Jessica – 'is at your school; he plays for the senior team. He says they are already talking about you as one of the best at St Joseph's.'

'Wow,' said Jerome. He felt stunned. Could this be true?

'Yes, mad, eh?' Lisa said. 'Erm … you'd better pay for your biscuits.'

Jerome turned towards the till to see a very unimpressed shopkeeper.

'Did you want to wait some more?' the shopkeeper asked.

'No, sorry,' said Jerome, and paid quickly. 'See you around,' he said to Lisa and Jessica.

'Lisa Stornoway,' she said. 'That's my full name. You can find me online. I mean, if you like.'

As the boys walked back to school, Darius nudged Jerome with his elbow.

'Girls are noticing you now,' he said.

'Shut up,' said Jerome.

'Jay-Jay Fifteen,' said Darius. 'We should turn that into a logo. And trademark it. My dad can sort that for you.'

'Shut up,' said Jerome.

'You are saying that now,' said Darius, 'but you'll thank

me in five years. And you can tell me not to talk about it, but you know that you like it.'

Jerome didn't say much for the rest of the walk home. He knew that he didn't just like it – he loved it.

As soon as he got back to his bedroom, Jerome sent a text to his mum.

> *Hey Mum, I hope you are OK. Want to speak to you tonight if you are free*

Sure. Sorry I can't talk more right now. Just a bit tied up at work

> *No I know you are busy, I just wanted to speak to you tonight, and to Ian if he is free*

Everything OK?

> *Yes everything is great. Just wanted to speak to you*

Not a problem, I'll
ask Ian. I know he
has been travelling

After a few minutes, Jerome's mum replied.

Just checked. Ian
can do 40 minutes
tonight at 6pm then
he has to go to an
event at Arsenal

*That's perfect,
thanks so much Mum.
We can do a video
chat. I'll send you
a link and you can
send it to Ian too*

Thank you. Love
you Jerome

Love you

That night, after dinner, Jerome sat in front of his laptop and opened up the video chat, waiting for his mum and for Ian to come online. His mum arrived first, her hair still tied up in a bun from work. She looked like she had just woken up.

'Hard day, Mum?' asked Jerome.

She smiled sadly. 'Do I look that bad?'

'No,' said Jerome. 'I'm sorry. I don't mean bad. Just very busy.'

'All my days are like that,' she said. Jerome heard someone talking loudly in the background.

'Dinner is in the same place as always, Larry,' she shouted back. 'It's on the cooker. Waiting for you.' She rolled her eyes.

'Larry is hungry again, then,' said Jerome.

'When is he not?' she said, and they both laughed.

A new window opened in the video chat, and Ian's face appeared.

'Good evening, all,' he said. He was wearing a black dinner suit, white shirt and black bow tie.

'Very smart this evening, Ian!' said Stephanie.

'Got to be,' he said. 'Going to an awards ceremony at the Emirates. They are doing an event for the staff. How you doing, Jerome?'

'Everything is amazing!' said Jerome. 'I was in the shop today and these two girls said they had seen one of my goals and it was so good that they were trying to copy how I scored it. And so many clubs have been watching me. There is even a rumour that Juventus are going to send someone.'

'Wow, Jerome,' said Ian. 'That's amazing. How are—'

'And they've moved me into the starting eleven

already,' interrupted Jerome, 'weeks before they said they would. I have already scored two goals in three games. Mr Baxter says I'm the most skilful attacker we have.'

'Jerome, that's great,' said Ian. 'I was—'

But Jerome cut him off before he could finish.

'Mr Baxter says I can play anywhere in the front three,' continued Jerome. 'Centre forward, right wide-forward, left wide-forward. I can play left wing or right wing. I have really been working on my left foot like you said and it's getting me a few assists.'

'Jerome, that's fantastic,' said Ian. 'I just—'

'When the scouts came and watched me,' said Jerome, 'I didn't talk to them because you are meant to let them just watch you quietly. But I know they were mostly watching me. And the way the girls are looking at me is different too. All of it is different. It's like – I have only been there for a few weeks but they are already treating me like I'm the man.'

Jerome stopped to take a breath before he said anything else but then he looked at Ian and his mum and he stopped talking completely. Their eyes and mouths were wide open.

'Ha, wow, Jerome,' said Ian. 'Have you finished?'

'Yes – yes, that's all,' said Jerome. 'Sorry.'

His mum didn't speak at first. Ian was smiling but she wasn't. Her eyebrows lowered themselves over her face like storm clouds. Her lips were tight and angry, like a wave which was rushing up the beach to smash a sandcastle. She put out a finger and tapped the screen of her laptop once, twice, three times.

'Thank goodness,' she said at last. 'My son's head has got so big that I thought the glass was going to break.'

'But Mum—'

'But Mum, nothing!' she said. 'Ian made time. I made time. To hear about your school and your studies. And all I hear is you boasting about girls and Juventus! Jerome, this is not you!'

Jerome looked at Ian for support, but Ian looked like he had just chewed a hot spice.

'Sorry, Mum,' he said. 'Sorry, Ian.'

'Jerome,' said Ian. 'We know you are excited. But it's like that song I was playing when you came to Uncle Ray's. Don't let it go to your head.'

'I didn't mean to,' said Jerome.

'We never mean to,' said Ian. 'It's very strange being a footballer. One day you are just working on the training ground with nobody watching you. And then the next day everyone is putting cameras and flashing lights in your face. When that happened to me at Crystal Palace, I couldn't deal with it. No one could tell me how to behave. I walked everywhere like I was a king. But I wasn't. You see what I'm saying?'

Jerome nodded.

'It all changes so fast in football and I'm happy it's changing so fast for you. We just need to be a bit calmer about it.'

'You're right,' said Jerome.

'Tell you what,' said Ian, 'why don't we meet for some food next Sunday lunchtime, about one o'clock. I'll come to Leytonstone; we can get a curry at this great restaurant I know, called Road to Kerala. Let's get some food there and we can just catch up on everything.'

'That sounds perfect,' said Jerome.

'Good, good,' said Stephanie. 'Now, Ian only has a few minutes left. So let's talk about the important things.' She paused. 'So, what marks are you getting in class?'

***

The next day, at his team's training session, Jerome tried to follow everything that Ian said. But there was one problem. Some of his own teammates were not happy with all the attention he was getting. When they played a practice match at the end of the session, three boys started kicking Jerome. The first one to kick Jerome was Eugene, who waited until Jerome's team had a corner, then stepped on his ankle. Jerome was about to scream, but then Eugene whispered a threat in his ear.

'If you say anything we will kick you harder next time. And don't you run telling the teachers like a scared little boy. Football is a man's game.'

Mr Baxter saw Jerome limping away and was worried.

'Jerome, are you OK?' he asked.

'Fine, sir,' said Jerome. 'I just ran a bit too hard at the start.'

The next person to kick Jerome was Stanley Warwick, who tripped him up when he was running to take a pass from Toby.

'Ref,' said Toby, 'didn't you see that?'

'I'm sorry,' said Mr Baxter, 'I was too far behind.' He ran over as quickly as he could to help Jerome up. Before he got there Stanley stood over Jerome and said, quickly and quietly, 'Look how everyone runs to help Wrighty's boy. Look at you, lying there like Ian Wright's little pet.'

The third kick came from Patrick McGinn, who waited till Jerome ran past him with the ball then hit him just above the knee. Mr Baxter saw this foul and ran straight over as Jerome rolled on the ground in agony.

'Patrick,' he said, 'get out of here. I'll be writing to your housemaster this evening. What a disgraceful tackle.'

But Patrick didn't care. He was already walking off the pitch, with a smirk on his face. 'Oh no,' he said to Eugene, as he walked away. 'Everyone is upset because I kicked Wrighty's pet.'

As Jerome held his left knee, he was surprised to see Gavin Bradley offering his hand to help him up. Weren't Stanley, Patrick and Eugene his best friends?

'Don't mind them,' said Gavin. 'That is their way of trying to toughen you up, but sometimes they take it too far. They need to remember that we are all teammates here.'

'Thanks, Gavin,' said Jerome.

'Sometimes,' said Gavin, 'people will go after you

because they are a little bit jealous. You just need to show them that Ian Wright is not the reason you are here. You need to prove to them that Jerome Jackson is his own man.'

'Oh I will,' said Jerome. He couldn't work out why Gavin was suddenly being so nice, but it was better than when Gavin was being mean to him. 'I will.'

That Sunday, as Jerome was getting ready to go out for lunch with Ian, he thought back to Monday's training session. He remembered the faces of Stanley, Patrick and Eugene as they attacked him, one after the other. He remembered their voices: *Wrighty's Pet. Wrighty's Pet. Wrighty's Pet.*

Just wait, thought Jerome. *After we've played our next match, they won't call me that any more.*

14

THE KING

'Jerome, what are you doing? That looks ridiculous.'

As Jerome unzipped his training top, Toby looked at his friend and sighed. He was wearing a black T-shirt with bright gold letters on the front. The letters spelled out the nickname that someone on the Internet had given him: JAY-JAY FIFTEEN.

'Darius got it made for me,' said Jerome, 'and I think it looks cool.'

'It looks cool,' said Toby, 'if you're a pop star. You're not a pop star, are you?'

'No need to be so sarcastic,' said Jerome. 'It's just a bit of fun.'

'Whatever,' said Toby. 'Anyway, where have you been recently? I haven't seen you around town much.'

'I've been hanging out in Dalston with Gavin.'

Toby stuck the tip of a finger in each of his ears and then took them out again, as if he was not sure he had heard Jerome properly.

'You? Hanging out with Gavin? Jerome, he can't stand you!'

'That's not true actually,' said Jerome. 'We had some trouble at first but that's only because we are both so competitive. But now we have got past that, and we get on really well. Plus, if we are going to play up front together, it's good that we get to know each other.'

'All you need to know about Gavin,' said Toby, 'is that he is not a nice person. All the Bradleys are like that. His parents, his big sister. They are very charming people, but they are very mean.'

'I met his big sister last week,' said Jerome, 'and she was awesome. Fit too.'

'There we go,' said Toby. 'Heidi Bradley strikes again.'

'Oh come on, Toby. Everyone fancies her,' said Jerome. 'She's the fittest girl at Queen Elizabeth's.'

'Not everyone fancies girls,' said Toby quickly. His voice stumbled and his cheeks went bright pink. He looked down at the floor.

'Oh – no, oh no, of course they don't,' said Jerome. 'Toby, that's OK if they don't.' He waited for Toby to look up, and when he did his friend was smiling again.

'Thank you, Jerome,' he said.

'When Uncle Ray was a boy, he didn't fancy girls either,' said Jerome.

'Who's Uncle Ray?'

'Oh, he owns the barbershop where I met Ian,' said Jerome.

'Ah, how is Wrighty doing?' asked Toby. 'My granddad was so excited about the video he made me. He can't stop talking about it.'

Jerome suddenly remembered that he had skipped his lunch meeting with Ian, and his stomach jumped with guilt.

'I haven't seen him for a little while,' said Jerome. 'I'm trying to do my own thing. I don't want to bother him all the time.'

'If I knew him,' said Toby, 'I definitely would.'

'You say that,' said Jerome, 'but it's different when you have a friend like that. People think you didn't earn what you have.'

Toby sighed again.

'Jerome,' he said, 'you are really going to have to get over that.'

Just then, they saw Mr Baxter walking over for the start of the training session, and Jerome quickly zipped up his training top, covering his T-shirt so Mr Baxter couldn't see it.

'I thought your T-shirt was just a bit of fun?' asked Toby, raising an eyebrow.

Jerome shook his head but said nothing.

That afternoon's class, a double geography lesson with Mr Saunders, was the slowest that Jerome could remember. He was suddenly finding school much more boring — all he could think about was the next football match. On the back page of his exercise book, he started counting down the hours to each game, leaving a thin black mark with his pen for each hour passed. Jerome wondered if he would one day be so famous that they would put him in a computer game. He wondered what scores they would give him. He would probably get 94 for pace, 93 for shooting, 93 for passing, 95 for dribbling, 57 for defending and 65 for physicality. He could work on his physicality and his defence for sure. At the end of his class he looked down at his exercise book and realized that he had not taken a single note! He hadn't even heard anything his teacher had said. He looked up at Mr Saunders and luckily, he hadn't noticed a thing. As Jerome left the classroom, he turned on his phone, and saw that he had two missed calls from his mum. He called her back at once.

'Hi Mum,' he said, 'everything OK?'

'Yes, yes,' she said. 'All fine. How are you?'

'I'm good, just working and training,' he said.

'Good, good,' she said. 'How was your lunch with Ian?'

Jerome gulped.

'Great,' he lied. 'Great.'

'That's nice,' she said. 'What did you talk about?'

Jerome was anxious now. Sometimes talking to his mum was like talking to one of the world's best detectives. If you didn't tell her the truth she could work it out in seconds. He had to think quickly.

'We talked about … just football stuff. How to stay sensible under pressure, how not to get distracted by success. How to score goals in big games.'

'Wonderful,' she said. 'How kind of him to give you so much of his time.'

'Yes, it was,' said Jerome. *Phew*, he thought, *she sounds happy with that.*

But his mum wasn't finished.

'What meal did you eat?' she asked.

'What do – I had curry,' spluttered Jerome. 'So did Ian.'

'What did you order?' she said. 'It was only three days ago. You've forgotten?'

'Oh, sorry, I can't remember. I've been stressed with school work,' said Jerome.

'Just trying to take care of your diet,' she said.

'Oh, of course,' said Jerome. 'Of course.'

She sounded satisfied with that. 'Well, I'd better get back to work,' she said. 'Love you.'

'Love you,' said Jerome. As soon as she hung up, he gasped with relief. He had not lied to his mum in years. He felt bad about ignoring Ian too, but he was just trying to make his own life. And he didn't want anyone calling him Wrighty's boy or Wrighty's pet any more.

Four days later, the morning after a great training session where he scored four goals in a practice match, Jerome got his best news so far at St Joseph's. He walked down to the school notice boards to see that he was in the starting eleven for the Junior Firsts. It was the first round of the UK Schools Cup, at home against Livingstone Academy. As he stood there smiling, he felt someone pat him on the back. He turned around, and there was Patrick McGinn.

'Welcome to the big time, Jerome,' he said.

'Ah – thanks,' said Jerome. 'Sorry, I'm just surprised that you sound happy for me.'

'Why would I not be happy for you?' asked Patrick.

'Because you have been kicking me for most of the last week.'

'That's just a test,' said Patrick. 'You're one of us now. You should call Wrighty and tell him the good news.'

'No,' said Jerome. 'He's not my dad. He can wait.'

Patrick smiled, as if he had heard what he wanted, and walked away. 'See you for the match tomorrow.'

'See you,' said Jerome. He looked down at his phone. Darius had opened a new Instagram account for him, @therealjayjay15, and it already had five hundred and nineteen followers. It only had one post up there: his goal against Hawkswell, which now had two hundred and thirty-seven thousand views. He took a picture of the team sheet, and uploaded it with the words, 'The journey continues.' Finally, he looked at the time on his phone: there were only twenty-nine hours until kick-off, and he was going to count down every single one.

***

Jerome had wished for this day with all his heart, and here he was. He was standing in the centre circle, next to Gavin Bradley, about to kick off the match for St Joseph's. He put his foot on top of the ball and he looked at the side of the pitch: there were more than three hundred people in the crowd, even more than the last time. He looked back at Kieran and Eugene in midfield, then back at Toby in defence, then all the way back to Billy in goal. He gave his team and the crowd a thumbs-up.

'How are you feeling?' asked Gavin. 'Big game today. Are you a bit nervous?'

'Nervous?' said Jerome. I'm feeling sorry for them.' He nodded towards his opponents. 'They are weak, I can see it. Look at them. Two central midfielders, standing too close to each other. Behind them, two central defenders, who are standing too far apart. When we get past them, we'll be laughing.'

Gavin puffed out his cheeks, a little surprised.

'Whoa, that's a bit cocky,' he said.

'Not cocky,' said Jerome, leaning towards Gavin. He covered his mouth with his hand, so no one could see what he was saying. 'Let's attack them at once.'

'I don't know about that,' said Gavin. 'Mr Baxter said we should start the game slowly and patiently. Those are the tactics he told us.'

'I know he said that,' said Jerome. 'But that's what Livingstone are expecting us to do. They're not ready for us. Trust me. When I give the ball to you from kick-off,

143

wait two seconds then hit it in the air straight back to me, then make sure you are running next to me, not more than five metres away. Trust me.'

'I thought I was the captain?' said Gavin.

'You are,' said Jerome. He took his hand away from his mouth. 'But this is the plan.'

The referee blew his whistle. Jerome rolled the ball with his studs to Gavin, then ran forward. The first midfielder ran towards Gavin to tackle him, leaving a space behind him. Gavin waited just like Jerome said: one second, two seconds – then he hit a perfect pass, floating over the head of the midfielder who was rushing towards him. By the time Jerome saw the ball coming from Gavin, he was almost at full speed. The second midfielder stepped forward, seeing the trouble, but it was too late. Instead of waiting for the ball to drop to his feet, Jerome jumped forward and headed it high over the next midfielder. All of a sudden, it was just him in front of the two central defenders. The crowd was loud as a forest fire, their voices tearing through the air like angry flames through dry trees, but Jerome could not hear any of them. All he could see was the ball dropping from the sky in front of him and the eyes of the two central defenders growing wider in fear as they saw him coming. He thought, *This is good, I have got you*, and then he moved up to full speed and headed the ball forward again, just over their heads, and he ran right between them just as they tried to close the gap. Now he was in the Livingstone penalty area, and the ball had not bounced yet, and only now, as he pulled his left foot back to shoot, did he let the ball fall all the way to the ground, and he brought his left foot forward with so much power, and the keeper dived down to his right to save it...

But Jerome didn't hit the ball hard, or towards goal. Instead, as the goalkeeper skidded along the ground and stopped just next to the goalpost, Jerome nudged the ball up and gently to his right, so that it floated through the air as slowly as a soap bubble. The ball fell right on to the forehead of Gavin, who had been running alongside Jerome all the way, and he thudded the ball into the net. 1–0 St Joseph's!

'Oh my God,' said Gavin, running towards Jerome to celebrate. 'Oh my God, that was incredible!'

But Jerome didn't even celebrate. He waved Gavin away, and ran straight back to the halfway line. 'That's a good start,' he yelled back to Gavin, 'but we are only just heating up!'

All along the sideline, members of the crowd held their heads in shock. Eleven seconds! Gavin had scored in just eleven seconds! Jerome looked back at his teammates and he even saw smiles on the faces of Stanley and Eugene. As Livingstone prepared to kick off again, he walked over to Gavin.

'They are even more worried now,' he said. 'They are going to stay tight so they are going to leave space open on the wings. That's where we can hit them next. When we get the ball, we play it back to Toby, then he can hit it wide. I'll be running for it. You be ready.'

'OK, General Jerome,' Gavin said with a smile. 'Whatever you say.'

He thought Jerome was just being bossy, but four minutes later everything happened exactly as Jerome said it would. Livingstone were so concerned about being a goal behind that they sent too many people forward, and that was when Jerome started to run over to the left wing, before St Joseph's even had the ball. As soon as Toby tackled their striker, he hit the ball hard and high to Jerome, who was all by himself on the halfway line, one yard from the crowd. He pushed the ball down the wing ahead of him, and then, when three defenders came to tackle him, he fired the ball forward, curving in a low, fast loop across the field, to the edge of the penalty area. The ball bounced once, twice, and there was Gavin, ready to meet it with his right foot, driving it low and firm past the goalkeeper's left hand. 2–0 to St Joseph's!

This time, when Gavin ran all the way over to Jerome, Jerome raised both his hands and gave him a high-five.

'I know they call you Jay-Jay,' said Gavin, 'but I'm going to start calling you General.'

'Works for me,' said Jerome. He glanced across at Mr Baxter, who was pointing to his piece of paper with the team's tactics, and then shrugging.

'I think we upset Sir,' said Jerome to Gavin.

'2–0 is a good excuse,' replied Gavin.

The rest of the game passed without much drama. St Joseph's played with the style that Mr Baxter had told them to, slow and patient, and Livingstone had some good attempts but they just couldn't score. The game finished 2–0, and although Gavin had scored both goals, afterwards everyone was talking about Jerome. Mr Baxter did not look happy, though.

'Jerome,' he said, 'I know that we won, but you need to listen to what I tell you. I gave you clear instructions about how to play. And one day just doing it your own way won't work.'

Jerome nodded, but he wasn't really listening. He couldn't stop thinking of the way people were chanting his name. Gavin called him General, but he was even better than that. Right now, at St Joseph's, he felt like he was the king.

15

WELCOME

Jerome lay back in his seat as the luxury minibus floated down the motorway and smiled. This vehicle was so comfortable that he felt like he was a member of the Royal Family. He had so much room for his legs that he could stretch them all the way out without touching the seat in front of him. He had his own table with enough space for his laptop, a bottle of water, and his book, but he was so excited that he didn't want to read anything. Gavin had invited him and some other friends to his house in Cornwall for the weekend, and Jerome couldn't wait to get there.

Their football team had no match that Saturday, and so they were allowed to leave school at midday. Gavin, Eugene and Jerome had waited with their bags at the gates of St Joseph's, and Gavin's driver had brought this beautiful silver vehicle up the road. Its body was as smooth and glistening as the skin of a great white shark, and everyone stopped to look as it rolled past. *Wow*, thought Jerome. *This is the big time.*

Archie, Gavin's driver, got out and slid open the side door of the minibus, and Jerome saw that there were five girls in there – Gavin's sister Heidi, and four of her friends from Queen Elizabeth's. When Heidi looked at him, she made his skin feel like it was burning. Just like Michelle used to.

'This is Veronique,' said Heidi, 'and this is Jenny, Sarah, and this is Yvonne.' Her friends smiled at them, then went back to their conversation. They all looked like they were going to a fashion show; they were wearing expensive dresses – one of them was even wearing a fancy white hat. Whenever they turned to look at the boys Jerome felt nervous and put his head down.

'Here, Jerome, you're over here,' said Archie. Jerome looked up and saw that there was an empty seat and table in front of him, and the table had a small white card with gold lettering on it. He leaned over to read it. *Reserved for Mr Jerome Jackson.* Jerome slid into his seat. It felt as soft as lying down in a bath filled with cotton wool. He looked at the seat in front and to his shock there was a television screen facing him.

'Gavin,' said Jerome, 'this thing has TVs, tables, tinted windows. Does it fly as well?'

Everybody laughed.

'Jerome,' said Heidi, turning to him. 'You are so, so funny. We are just going to have the best time this weekend.'

Jerome was so embarrassed by her kind words that he didn't speak for several minutes after that. As the minibus glided through the middle of London, he saw his phone humming on his table, showing a number he didn't recognize. He was so cosy in his seat that he didn't put it to his ear, he just pressed answer, and was startled when he heard the voice coming out of the speaker.

'Jerome? Is that you?'

Oh my God, thought Jerome. The voice was so familiar that several people on the minibus recognized it at once. Gavin's head poked round the corner of his seat.

'Is that Ian Wright calling you?'

Jerome nodded and quickly put the phone to his ear.

Ian continued to chat. 'How are you doing, man? I've been worrying about you. Your mum gave me your number – I wouldn't normally call but I wanted to check in. Are you OK?'

'Of course I'm OK,' said Jerome, a little flustered. He was still feeling guilty about abandoning Ian at lunch.

'Hey. Didn't mean to annoy you. After you missed lunch, I just wondered if you were avoiding me. Or having a hard time.'

'I'm having a great time,' he replied. 'Everything's perfect.'

'What's the matter, Jerome?'

'Nothing!' snapped Jerome.

'Hey,' said Ian. His voice was quiet and gentle, as if he was worried that speaking too loudly would scare Jerome away. 'I only wanted to be sure.'

'I'm good. I'm really good. I've got to go. I'm with some friends. And reception is really bad anyway, so it is hard for me to talk.' Jerome looked up and saw that most of his fellow passengers on the minibus were looking at him. 'And you don't need to keep checking on me. You're not my dad!'

And then Jerome hung up.

There were eight seconds of silence until Gavin spoke.

'Whoa, Jerome,' he said, sounding impressed. 'That was cold. You just told a whole football legend where to go.'

'*Ice* cold,' agreed Eugene.

'I'm nobody's boy,' said Jerome. He folded his arms and stared out the window as the sun began to break through the clouds. He pressed his elbows against his stomach and tried not to think of the hurt in Ian's voice. He turned his phone on silent and watched it vibrate twice before it stopped. Finally it buzzed and a simple message arrived from Ian.

```
Always here if
you need me.
```

Jerome turned his face all the way towards the curtain and pulled his hoodie over his head, pretending to be sleeping. That way, nobody on the bus could see the shame on his face.

Jerome woke to the sound of tapping on the window. He opened his eyes to see everyone else standing outside on a gravel path, their luggage by their feet. Jerome scrambled outside to join them.

'Sleepy made it at last,' said Gavin. 'Welcome to Middleburgh Hall. And our parents are away for the weekend, so it's all ours.'

Jerome looked around and almost gasped. Two hundred metres away, next to the gates of the estate they had just entered, was a house as big as the largest ones in Hackney. Halfway down the drive was a bridge over a lake, which disappeared into the forest on either side. And behind him was the Bradleys' family home, which was twice the size of the main building at St Joseph's.

'Gavin, you live in *there*?' asked Jerome.

'Oh, only in the holidays,' said Gavin. 'The rest of the time, I stay at our family's place in London.'

'Do you not get lost in this house?' Jerome shook his head.

Gavin laughed. 'You find your way round,' he said, 'after a few years. Dinner at six o'clock. See you in a bit.'

Gavin was not joking – the house was so big that his family had even built a smartphone app for visitors, in case they couldn't work out where they were. It had two swimming pools, one indoors and one outdoors, three dining rooms, a library, a gym and a cinema. It needed twelve people to work there and take care of it, including a chef and a gardener and of course the driver, Archie, and they all lived in the house near the gates. Martina, the head of house, showed Jerome to one of the countless bedrooms. The bedroom had its own bathroom and shower and there was a suit laid out on the bed in Jerome's size, for him to wear to dinner that evening. He had to ask Martina to help him put on his bow tie, and when he was ready, he sent his mum a selfie.

Look at these threads Mum

Very dashing! But I thought you said you were going to your friend's house?

I'm at my friend's house

Ah. It's just that it looks like you went to the 1930s

Very funny Mum

Ian said he
called you

                              Yeah

He said you
sounded busy

                       Yeah and there
                           wasn't good
                            reception

You're OK though?

                        Yeah I'm great
                              thanks

Love you

                            Love you

Everyone else had been to the house before, so they
had gathered in the dining room before Jerome found it.
When he walked in, they were all seated around a vast
table, and the only empty seat was between Gavin and
Heidi. He couldn't believe how smart everyone looked –
like characters from a film.

'Here you go, Jerome,' said Heidi, pulling back his

chair for him. 'You have pride of place.' Jerome sat down awkwardly, sensing that everyone's eyes were on him. He had eaten one or two fancy dinners before but this was something else. He wasn't sure how to eat some of the food – he had never had oysters or lobsters before – so he watched the others and copied them. He wasn't very good at it, so he ended up spilling some food over himself. He heard someone laugh at him but this time the laughter was not friendly. It took him a long time to eat and when he was finished everyone else was already looking bored.

'Sorry,' he said. 'And I ruined my suit.' He felt so embarrassed.

'You didn't ruin anything,' said Gavin. 'And no need to apologize. That wasn't bad for your first time. Eating all that stuff is fiddly.'

'I give him a three out of ten,' said Veronique.

'That's generous,' said Sarah.

'No need to be mean,' Heidi said.

Veronique and Sarah rolled their eyes.

'Jerome,' said Yvonne, 'what do your parents do?'

'It's just me and my mum,' said Jerome. 'My dad—'

'Oh, he left you and your mum?' asked Yvonne. 'How awful.'

'Kind of,' said Jerome. 'He died.'

'Oh, how dreadful,' said Yvonne. Her cheeks turned bright pink.

'What does your mum do?' asked Jenny.

'She works in catering,' said Jerome.

'You can't buy much lobster doing work like that,' said Jenny.

'Jenny!' said Heidi.

'Not sure why everyone is roasting Jerome all of a sudden,' said Gavin. He turned to Jerome. 'I'm sorry. Sometimes their banter goes a bit far.'

It doesn't feel like banter, thought Jerome.

'I say we all go to the hot tubs,' said Heidi. 'We can get the staff to bring us some cool drinks. Everyone get their bathing suits on; see you down there in an hour.' She saw that Jerome was looking hesitant. 'Oh, come on,' she said, patting his arm, and he felt a surge of heat go through it.

'OK,' he said.

The hot tubs were on the ground floor at the back of the house, a long walk from Jerome's bedroom. The room they were in had a glass wall which looked out on to the lawn, which stretched away for ever into the darkness. The eight of them got into the largest tub, right next to the window, and after a little awkwardness Jerome relaxed. *This is more like it*, he thought. Heidi smiled at him. *My God, what if she likes me?!* The thought was both scary and exciting.

Half an hour after they had all settled down, Martina came into the room, looking anxious. She leaned next to Gavin and spoke to him quietly, but Jerome could still hear her.

'Gavin, your grandparents have just arrived from the south of France.'

'Oh lovely,' he said. 'They said they might drop in.'

'But you should have warned me,' whispered Martina. 'I didn't know they were in town this weekend.'

'I'm sure they will be fine, Martina,' said Gavin. 'Their room is always prepared. And Francois can cook them something.'

'But Gavin,' said Martina, then she paused. 'You know what they think of, well...' She looked at Jerome very quickly, but not quickly enough that he didn't notice. *What did she mean by that?* thought Jerome.

'It will be fine,' said Gavin.

'Is everyone decent?' bellowed a voice from outside. 'I'm coming in!'

The door swung open and there they were: Lord and Lady Middleburgh, Gavin and Heidi's grandparents. Only they couldn't really see Lady Middleburgh because Lord Middleburgh was standing in front of her in the doorway, his red jacket bright as a small sun, his silver hair quivering as he looked around the room. He saw them all sitting in the hot tub and his eyes fixed upon Jerome at once.

'What is *he* doing here?' He pointed at Jerome.

A couple of the girls gasped.

Wait, thought Jerome, *is he talking about me?*

'Get out of there,' said Lord Middleburgh. 'Martina, tell him to get out. And make sure you clean the hot tub tomorrow.'

No one said anything.

Finally Jerome said, 'I can't believe this is happening. You're making me feel like my body is dirty.'

He felt his skin roasting under their eyes and all of a sudden he was crying, sobbing all by himself in the middle of the hot tub while everyone just watched him. 'I just wanted a nice time. This has been so horrible. Why did you even ask me here? I want to go home.'

'We can arrange that first thing tomorrow,' said Lord Middleburgh.

Jerome stood up, surrounded by silence, and took his dressing gown from the hook near the door. Lord Middleburgh held the door open for him, and Jerome walked through. He did not once look back.

***

Jerome woke up at seven the next morning and at first he didn't remember anything of the night before. But then the memories came charging back, and he found himself shivering with unhappiness. Yesterday had been one of the worst days of his life. It felt like they were bullying him the second he arrived at Middleburgh Hall. Everyone was being mean, judging him, making fun of the way he ate or of his family or of the way he looked. And calling his skin dirty was the worst. Jerome had never hated the colour of his skin but now he felt like he was a piece of rubbish they thought they could throw by the side of the road. Even Larry had never made him feel this bad.

He packed his things and walked downstairs to the driveway, where Archie was waiting in a small black car. He looked as embarrassed as Martina had the night before.

'I'm so sorry about this, Jerome,' he said. 'Martina told me everything. You're a nice boy and you didn't deserve this.' He got out and held the back door open for Jerome, and then they drove out through the gates. 'Lord Middleburgh told me I was to drive you to the local station and buy you a ticket to London,' said Archie, 'but I'll drive you halfway to London instead, then put you on a train from there. That's as far as I can go, because I have work later today, but I don't want to leave you here in the middle of nowhere.'

'They treated me like I was rubbish, just nothing. Not even a person,' said Jerome.

'It's not right; it's not right,' said Archie.

'You know what,' said Jerome. 'You can leave me right here, near the local station.'

'But Jerome—'

'Just do it,' said Jerome. 'Right here.' His voice was cold now.

'OK, OK,' said Archie gently. He turned off the main road and stopped the car at the top of the station car park. Jerome strode off at once and didn't look back.

'Good luck, Jerome,' Archie called after him, and then he drove away.

16

A BIG MISTAKE

Jerome was so upset about his stay at Gavin's house that he couldn't sleep on Sunday night. But he was also so embarrassed by it that he didn't tell anyone else. The next day, just before the beginning of training, he walked up to Gavin, full of anger. Gavin was standing next to Eugene, getting ready to do some passing exercises, and as they saw Jerome approach they looked up and waved.

'Hey, Jerome,' said Gavin, before he could speak. 'How was your train journey back?'

'My journey?' said Jerome. He was confused now. 'It was you who made me—'

'The train journey is about five hours from Cornwall to Paddington,' interrupted Gavin. 'Then you have to get all the way across town to East London. It must have taken you ages.'

'You must be so tired,' added Eugene.

'Gavin,' said Jerome. He had to pause then, because to his horror his eyes were filling with tears. He rubbed his eyes with his sleeves quickly, but Gavin had already seen his sadness.

'You're looking very sensitive there, Jerome,' said Gavin.

'What your granddad did to me,' said Jerome, 'what you allowed him to do to me – that's one of the worst things that has ever happened to me in my life.'

'I don't know what you're talking about,' said Gavin, looking serious all of a sudden. 'Eugene,' he said, 'what is Jerome talking about?'

Eugene shrugged. 'I have no idea.'

'Did anything even happen?' asked Gavin.

'Gavin—' Jerome began to speak, but Gavin put up his hand and Jerome stopped.

'Hush, Jerome,' said Gavin. 'You sound like someone who is getting ready to go and tell a teacher a story. But what if no one else saw the story you tell them about? What if the teacher doesn't believe you? St Joseph's is a very big and very lonely place for students who spread lies about other students.'

Jerome looked at Gavin and then at Eugene and then back at Gavin.

'You planned all of this, didn't you?' he said.

'Like I said,' said Gavin, 'I don't know what you're talking about.' He was smiling now. This had been a game, and he had won.

That afternoon's training session was Jerome's worst since he had come to St Joseph's. In fact, it was the worst football he had played in many years. Every time Jerome's teammates gave the ball to him, he stuck out his leg clumsily and the ball bounced away. He couldn't control the easiest of passes. Every time he shot the ball towards goal, it went high over the bar or far wide of the posts. He was playing so badly that Mr Baxter actually stopped the game and took him to one side.

'Jerome,' he asked, 'are you OK? I know there's a big match tomorrow – it's normal to be nervous.'

But Jerome wasn't thinking about the big match. All he could think of was the face and voice of Gavin's granddad. He held his stomach with both hands and he thought he was going to be sick.

'Is it OK if I leave early?' he asked Mr Baxter. 'I'm not feeling too well.'

'Of course, Jerome, of course,' he replied. 'Make sure you go straight to the school doctor, OK?'

Jerome nodded and walked away slowly, still clutching his stomach. He thought he could hear Gavin laughing quietly as he left the training ground, and as soon as he got round the corner he bent over near a hedge and vomited. And again he heard the voice of Gavin's granddad in his head.

Maybe Gavin's granddad was right, thought Jerome. *Maybe people like me don't belong in a house like his.* He looked around at the big expensive school buildings, and then thought of the small cheap flat where he lived with his mum and Larry. *Maybe people like me don't belong in a school like St Joseph's.* And that's when Jerome made a big mistake.

He didn't go to the school doctor, as he had promised. And he didn't go to class that afternoon. Instead, he walked out of school and went and sat down in a local cafe, sipping a huge mug of hot chocolate and staring out of the window at the cars rolling past. He didn't want to study any more textbooks or kick any footballs. He didn't want to see anyone from St Joseph's ever again. He just wanted to go home to his mum and shut his bedroom door and forget everything. The hot chocolate, which was thick as tomato soup, soothed his chest as it went down his throat. Jerome leaned his head against the window, and soon he was asleep.

Tap! Tap!

Jerome woke up to see someone's hand tapping on his coffee table. He looked up to see the barista who had served him his hot chocolate. He was frowning at Jerome, his eyebrows rising over the rims of his brown glasses.

'Sorry to disturb you,' said the man, 'but is your name Jerome Jackson?'

Jerome stretched his arms above his head and yawned. 'Yes,' he said. The sugar in that drink was so strong. His eyes still felt so heavy.

'Thank goodness,' the barista said. 'Your school is so worried about you. Everyone's been looking for you.

One of your teachers just called the cafe. They've been calling all the local shops to see if anyone has seen you.'

'Oh my God,' said Jerome. He was suddenly wide awake and he felt sick again. 'Oh no. What's the time?' He looked down at his phone. It was almost six o'clock. He had been sleeping for three hours!

'Please, please go back as quickly as you can,' said the man. 'I'll let them know you're here, so they know you're fine.'

'They're going to kill me,' said Jerome.

'It's going to be OK,' said the man, but his voice didn't sound like it was going to be OK. Jerome dropped four pound coins on the table to pay for his drink – it was too much, but he didn't care – and before the man could say anything else he was already out of the door, and running towards the gates of St Joseph's.

As soon as Jerome got back to his boarding house he knew that he was in big, big trouble. The first two boys who saw him just shook their heads and walked past. Oskar, one of the boys in the year above, simply said, 'You had better go and see Mr Franklin at once. He is waiting for you.'

By the time Jerome reached Mr Franklin's office, he was trembling. When he walked through the door, he saw that Mr Franklin was so angry that he could not even sit down. He was walking up and down the room with his hands behind his back. As soon as he saw Jerome enter, he turned towards him and roared.

'Where do you think you have been?'

'Mr Franklin, I'm so sorry, I—'

'We have rules here, Jerome!' said Mr Franklin. 'At St Joseph's, we don't just go wandering off when we feel like it!'

'I didn't mean to cause trouble,' said Jerome. 'I'm so sorry.'

'We have been running all over town looking for you!' shouted Mr Franklin. 'I was about to call your poor mother but I didn't want to worry her at work. What do you think you were doing?'

Jerome thought about the weekend at Gavin's house but he was too ashamed to tell Mr Franklin.

'I was having a difficult time at football training,' he replied. 'I was so stressed out that I couldn't go to class. I just had to go and sit somewhere quiet to calm down.'

'Jerome.' Mr Franklin was speaking more quietly now, but he sounded as if he was more angry. 'It's one thing to have a bad time on the football pitch. But if you have a bad game, you don't just storm off without telling anyone where you are going. There are more important things than football.'

'I know that,' said Jerome sadly.

'Well, you don't behave like it,' said Mr Franklin. 'I have recommended to the headmaster that you should go home tomorrow morning and stay at home for a week. He agrees with me.'

Jerome imagined his mother's reaction. He thought

of the pain and the sadness that would cross her face when she saw that he had been sent away for breaking the rules.

'Please, no,' begged Jerome. 'I'll do extra studies. I'll do detention, anything. Please just don't send me home.'

'I'm afraid the decision has already been made,' said Mr Franklin. 'Students have been expelled for behaviour like this. The only reason you are not being punished more is because until now you have shown good discipline. But if you do anything like this again, your punishment will be more severe. You will go home first thing tomorrow morning. We will send you by taxi to make sure that you get there.'

'I understand,' said Jerome. He could see that he was not going to change Mr Franklin's mind. But then he remembered something, and he started to panic. 'But Mr Franklin,' he said. 'What about our football match tomorrow? It's a huge game and lots of scouts will be there from the big clubs! If I get sent home I'll miss it!'

'Yes, you will,' said Mr Franklin. 'Of course you will.'

'But, Mr Franklin, that's not fair!' *Why is this happening to me*, thought Jerome. *What have I done wrong?*

'Not fair!' Mr Franklin became loud again. 'I'll tell you what is not fair! It is not fair to have everyone running round after you because they think you have run away! There is more to life than football, Jerome. There are manners and there is good behaviour! That is what we teach here. Do you like what we teach here?'

'Yes, yes, sir,' said Jerome quickly.

'Then go to your room,' said Mr Franklin, 'and stay up there until tomorrow. Is that understood?'

'Yes, Mr Franklin,' said Jerome. He ran from the room, his eyes burning with tears.

***

The next afternoon was St Joseph's biggest game of the season, at home against Ryman High School. Ryman had beaten them last year in the semi-finals, and so St Joseph's were looking for revenge. But it was going to be a very tough contest. Ryman had not lost a game all season, and there was a rumour that Liverpool's academy was looking at two of their players. There was a crowd of about four hundred people to watch the game – boys from St Joseph's, girls from Queen Elizabeth's, and somewhere in there, a growing number of scouts. Just before kick-off, there was a murmur at the back of the crowd, and a few people turned around to see what the fuss was about.

'That's Ian Wright,' whispered one of them.

Ian, who was standing a few metres back from the crowd, pretended not to hear them. He was waiting to see Jerome. He had heard that Jerome was playing so well for St Joseph's, and so he had come to watch him as a surprise. But as he watched the players run out on to the field to warm up, he became more and more worried. He couldn't see Jerome anywhere, not in the starting eleven, not standing with the substitutes. Eventually, he stepped forward and tapped one of the members of the crowd on the arm.

'Excuse me,' he said to the man in front of him. 'Excuse me—'

'Wrighty! I knew it was you!' said the man. 'I used to come watch you with my dad! Do you remember that time in the FA Cup when you scored against Nottingham Forest? 1993, I think it was – my goodness, that's taking me back in time. The lad Mark Crossley was in goal for them. Good player but you gave him no chance. Great goal.'

'Hey, yes, I remember it well,' said Ian. 'Decent team, Forest. We did well to beat them that year. I was just wondering—'

'Could I have a selfie with you?' asked the man. 'Just for me to show my boys. Would you mind?'

'No problem,' said Ian. 'I just—'

'Just a minute, Wrighty, sorry,' said the man. He reached into his pocket for his smartphone and turned it on, waiting for it to load up. 'There.' He pressed his shoulder against Ian's, raised the smartphone in front of their faces, smiled and pushed his finger down. 'Got it. Thanks so much, Wrighty.'

'Glad to help,' said Ian. 'I was wondering,' he said quickly, 'do you know where Jerome Jackson is?'

'Oh, you don't know?' asked the man. 'He's not playing today. It was a big shock to everyone; there are some big clubs here to see him. I don't mind too much, because I'm a parent of one of the Ryman boys, so we have a much better chance of winning if he's not playing. But I was looking forward to seeing what all the fuss is about.'

Ian thanked the man and began walking away.

'Hey,' said the man, 'aren't you staying for the game?'

Ian didn't hear him, or the excited crowd, because all he could hear was his own thoughts. *What's going on, Jerome?* wondered Ian. *What's going wrong?*

PART 3

JUST FINE

17

IN TROUBLE

Jerome didn't want to go near his smartphone. He had turned it off and left it on the other side of his bedroom, face down. He didn't want to leave his flat in case he bumped into anyone he knew from his neighbourhood. He didn't want to see Larry and he was too embarrassed to look at his mum. He had not felt this bad since that day three years ago when he realized that his dad was never going to come home again.

The hardest thing for Jerome was when he had to tell his mum that his school had sent him home. He would never forget her face. She had come home from work later than usual, and sat down on the sofa, so tired from hours of cooking. She looked so tired that Larry even got up to make her a cup of tea. And then Jerome walked into the living room and she looked at him in surprise and asked why he wasn't at school. Larry didn't say anything, and so Jerome had to say: 'Mum, I got in trouble for not going to class, and so my teachers sent me home for a week.'

'Why didn't you go to class?' Stephanie asked, suddenly awake. 'Jerome, I told you there is nothing more important than school! Even if you get injured and you can never play football again, you will always have your education.' She turned to her boyfriend on the sofa. 'Look how hard Larry has to work because he didn't finish school!'

'Leave me out of this,' Larry replied.

'Larry, I'm not trying to be mean. I'm just saying it has been so hard for you,' she said.

'Mum, you finished all your school, and you still have to work so hard,' said Jerome.

'Jerome!' screamed Stephanie. He had never heard her so loud. 'Don't answer back to me! Your school kicked you out! Don't you dare tell me about finishing anything. You couldn't even finish one term without getting in trouble!'

Even Larry looked scared when she said that.

'So why did you decide not to go to class, Jerome?' asked Stephanie. 'Was it because you were hanging out with your friends? Or were you chasing a girl?'

Jerome sat there and thought about the horrible weekend at Gavin's house in Cornwall. He thought about spilling food everywhere on Gavin's nice table. He thought about Gavin's grandfather telling him to get out of the hot tub in front of everyone. He thought about everyone just standing there and watching him, no one saying anything to help him. He thought about how Gavin's granddad made him feel disgusting and dirty, like a piece of horse manure. He felt so, so ashamed. He never wanted to think about it again.

'I was chasing a girl,' he told Stephanie. 'Instead of going to class, I went to meet her. I was waiting for her at the cafe but she didn't turn up.'

'Jerome,' said Stephanie, 'I can't believe you would do a thing like that!'

'Well I did,' said Jerome. 'I did. I got tired of always going to school and being told what to do. Rules, rules, rules, all the time! I just wanted to do something for myself!'

'Jerome, what has got into you? I'm shocked!' said Stephanie. 'You sound so selfish! What will Ian think when I tell him? What is he going to say? He is trying so hard to help you and you are behaving like this.'

'Oh no, please don't tell Ian,' Jerome pleaded. 'I'll be back at school in just a few days. He doesn't have to know!'

'Of course I'll have to tell Ian!' said Stephanie. 'Jerome, you have let us down. What happened? You were doing so well!'

Jerome put his head in his hands. 'Oh, Mum I'm so sorry,' he said. 'I couldn't help it. It was too hard; I just couldn't go into class!'

'So it wasn't a girl?'

'No,' said Jerome. 'I can't tell you why I was struggling. I feel so stupid.'

'Then why did you lie to me just now?' asked Stephanie. 'Why did you lie?'

'I didn't know what else to say,' said Jerome. 'Please Mum, I'm so sorry, I just can't do it!'

Stephanie heard so much sadness in her son's voice that all her anger left her.

'OK, OK,' she said. 'You go and get some rest now, Jerome. It's been a difficult day for you, I can see that. Let's talk about this a little bit later. Maybe tomorrow.'

That conversation was two days ago, and they hadn't talked about it again. They just hadn't had time. Jerome's mum had been too busy at work, and Larry, for some reason, was not speaking to Jerome. He would see Jerome in the living room, stare at him, then turn away and carry on watching television.

But Jerome didn't mind. He didn't want to talk to anyone. To try to stop himself from feeling so sad that afternoon, he decided to go for a walk. Before he left the flat he made sure that he pulled his hood forward over his head, so that no one could see his face. He didn't want anyone to notice him and ask how school was going. He opened the door and went quickly down the hallway and then down the steps to the courtyard in front of his building. He didn't go quickly enough, though, because Mrs Malone saw him.

'Jerome? Little Tin, is that you?'

He ignored her and kept going. She called him one more time, and this time he heard the disappointment in her voice, and then she went quiet. Instead of turning right out of the courtyard, towards the high street, Jerome turned left towards the railway bridge, which led to the quieter part of town. When he got to the bridge, he stopped just under it, feeling safe in the darkness. He took his headphones from his pocket, stuffed them into his ears, and turned on his phone for the first time in two days.

As soon as he did that, he saw that his inbox was bulging with dozens of new text messages and voicemails, from people who were looking for him. He turned his phone to flight mode at once so he wouldn't have to read them, selected an album, and pressed play. The drums of 'Common Sense' by J Hus exploded into his ears as he started to walk. He kept his eyes on the pavement, the grey houses rumbling past him on either side as he strode along. He was feeling a little better until he got to the corner of a familiar street and then looked up to see Ijeoma's House, where he and his mum had had that first lovely meal with Ian.

Ian! Oh no. Jerome was so scared to speak to him. He must be feeling so let down. *Jerome, you are so stupid*, he thought. *How many boys would dream of Ian Wright helping them to become a footballer? Why did you have to go and mess it all up?* He looked down at his phone and he saw that he had a text message from Ian but he didn't want to read it. *He must be so angry at you*, he thought. *First you didn't see him when he came to meet you at that curry house, now you are ignoring him.* He turned up the music, trying to block out his thoughts, but even that didn't work. He pressed stop and turned to walk home.

As he entered the courtyard, he looked up at his apartment block. Mrs Malone was leaning over her balcony and she was looking straight at him.

'I knew it was you, Little Tin!' she yelled. 'I was calling you!'

'I'm sorry, Mrs Malone,' said Jerome. 'I didn't hear you. I was listening to my music.' He pointed to his earphones.

'Oh, OK!' she said. 'I was worried that you didn't want to talk to me!'

Now Jerome felt bad that he had lied to her.

'No, never,' he said. 'It's always nice to see you. How have you been?'

'Oh, I'm well, you know me! Just getting on with life. But how about you? How come you're back from school already? Didn't you just have your holidays?' she asked.

'I – I was having a bit of a fever, so they let me come home for a couple of days,' said Jerome. 'They didn't want anyone else in the football team to catch it.'

'Oh,' said Mrs Malone. 'Well I should get indoors then; I mustn't catch it from you. I haven't been feeling too good lately. Please do come and say hello when you are feeling better. It will be so lovely to hear all your news. I can't wait to tell all my friends about Jerome the big footballer!' She smiled and waved, and stepped back from the balcony, back into her flat.

Jerome stood alone in the courtyard and felt his stomach jump with shame. He had never ignored Mrs Malone before or lied to her, and now he had done both of those things in just half an hour. He trudged up the stairs full of sorrow. *What's wrong with you, Jerome?* he asked himself.

He unlocked the front door of his flat and kicked off his shoes in the hallway, dragging his coat slowly from his shoulders. He was about to shuffle into his bedroom when Larry called out to him from the living room.

'Oi, Jerome. Come in here for a minute.'

Jerome walked round the corner, where he saw Larry sitting on the sofa as usual, his legs planted wide apart.

'Sit down over there, I need to talk to you.'

Jerome sat up in the closest armchair, his shoulders high and his back straight.

'Good,' said Larry. 'At least you are still listening to some of us adults.'

Jerome frowned but said nothing.

'You know what this is?' asked Larry, raising his left leg in the air, and pointing to the back of it, just beneath his calf. He waited, and Jerome said nothing. 'Go on, you can do it.'

'It's the Achilles tendon,' said Jerome.

'Very good,' said Larry. 'Remember that for later.' He lowered his leg to the ground. 'When I was thirteen,' he said, 'I was one of the best hurdlers in my age group in the country. I was winning competitions everywhere. Not just all over London or even the Midlands. My dad would drive me up North and I would win competitions up there. Sunderland, Liverpool, you name it. I went to the national championships one year and came third. I had the quickest time that year. I should have won, mind you.' He pointed at his left leg again. 'And then, at the start of the new season, this. Let me tell you, Jerome, you never, ever want to snap your Achilles tendon. It is the worst pain I ever felt in my life. I was only thirteen when I did it, but the surgeon said it was the worst injury he had ever seen. It never really healed properly and the next season I tore it again. And then I was done. Fourteen years old, the fastest hurdler in the country, and I never competed again.'

'Larry, I never knew that,' said Jerome. 'I'm so sorry.'

'Are you sorry, though?' asked Larry. 'Because I see you come sulking in here every day, and I think, if I had the talent of this boy then I would already be famous. But you want everything easy, Jerome. You want everyone to sit there and clap for you whatever you do.'

'No, I don't,' said Jerome. 'It's not like that, I promise.'

'It is like that, Jerome,' said Larry. 'You are scared to test yourself. You don't get to play for Liverpool or Chelsea, so you run and play for your little church team for years. And then the moment you get a chance to live your dream, the moment you get a famous friend who gets you into a fancy school, you run away from it again.'

'That's not fair,' said Jerome. He thought about being in the hot tub. He thought of Gavin's granddad.

'Are you calling me a liar?' asked Larry.

'No, Larry, no, I'm not,' said Jerome.

'Look at me when you're calling me a liar,' said Larry, and Jerome looked at him, and then the fear came and suddenly Jerome's stomach began to tumble.

'Larry, I feel sick. I need to go to the toilet,' Jerome said urgently. He was afraid he was going to vomit.

'You're the liar,' said Larry, as Jerome rushed from the room. 'There's nothing wrong with you. Go on, run away again, Jerome! Just like you always do.'

18

GONE

That night Jerome could not get to sleep. He lay on his back in the dark and tried to relax but he just couldn't do it. Every time he closed his eyes his brain would say something mean to him and his eyes would open again in shock. His brain would tell him:

You are too scared to be a footballer, Jerome.

You are a coward; that's why you ran away from school, Jerome.

If you cared about your mum you would have stayed in school, Jerome.

At first Jerome tried to fight these words, he tried to push them away – *no, that's true*, he told himself, *no, that's not true* – but after a while he was just too tired, and he let all the bad thoughts swim around and around in his head until he believed them. *I was scared*, he told himself.

I was selfish, he told himself. *I don't even know if anyone wants me here any more.*

Jerome rolled on to his side, reached for his phone, and turned it on. It was just past four o'clock in the morning. He saw that he had even more text messages but he didn't check any of them. Instead, he opened one of the apps on his phone which showed him how much money he had in his bank account. He looked online and looked at two other websites, first for trains, then for hotels. Then he sat up in bed and he listened for any sound, but he heard nothing – his mum and Larry were still asleep. So he turned on the torch on his phone and slowly climbed out of bed and walked quietly towards his wardrobe. He put some clothes into a rucksack – two pairs of underwear, two T-shirts, two pairs of socks. After dressing in his favourite tracksuit, he walked out into the hallway and picked up his trainers, walking on tiptoes in his socks. He opened the front door of his flat, stepped through and closed it gently behind him. He sat down on the cool stone of the corridor outside, pressing his back against the wall as he slipped on his trainers. Then he stood up, slid his rucksack on to his back, and he ran.

***

Two hours later, Stephanie went to check on Jerome before going to work. The moment that she opened the door to his bedroom, she knew that Jerome had run away.

She didn't expect to find him inside there, because he often left the flat early in the morning for a run, but this felt different. His bedroom looked lonely and sad, like a tree in autumn that had just lost all its leaves.

'Larry!' she called. 'Larry!' She turned and strode down the short hallway towards her own bedroom, where her boyfriend was still sleeping. 'Jerome has gone!'

Larry rubbed his eyes. 'What do you mean?' he said. It was still too early for a conversation this loud.

'He's run away!' said Stephanie. 'I'm going to call the police!'

'Stop being so dramatic,' said Larry. 'He's probably just gone out for a wander.'

'I know my son!' said Stephanie. 'He has gone!' She reached for her smartphone to turn it on and make a call, but Larry took it from her hand.

'He hasn't run away,' said Larry slowly, getting out of bed and holding the phone high over her head so she couldn't reach it.

'Give me my phone!' yelled Stephanie.

'Not until you calm down,' said Larry.

'It was you, wasn't it?' asked Stephanie.

'What are you talking about?'

'It was you! You must have said something to him last night! What did you tell him?'

'Nothing I haven't told him before.'

'Larry Reynolds, if I find out that you made my son leave his own home in the middle of the night—'

Larry sneered. 'What will you do, Stephanie? What will you do? Kick me out? I don't think you will. Do you want me to tell you why?'

'Larry, stop—'

'You won't kick me out,' said Larry, 'because nobody else wants you.'

'Larry, please,' said Stephanie.

'Who will take you if I leave?' asked Larry. He was smiling but his face was not kind. 'Everyone will say that Stephanie Jackson can't keep a man,' said Larry. 'They will say that Stephanie's men leave her. They will say that she couldn't keep Martin and she couldn't keep Larry. Who will want to come and live in a flat with a sad mother and her angry boy?'

'Oh, Larry,' said Stephanie. She sat down on her bed and she put her face in her hands. When she took her hands away again she was crying. 'Why do you have to say such cruel things?' She took a tissue from her pocket and rubbed her eyes. 'What happened to the old Larry? The Larry who used to take me and Jerome to the beach? When we used to walk in the sand and laugh about silly things? What happened to him? Why don't you behave like that any more?'

'Because the old Larry was soft,' said Larry. 'He didn't give you and Jerome enough rules. And that's what you both need in this flat. The new Larry is better for all of us. Here,' he said, putting an arm around her, waiting for her to stop crying. 'Here's your phone. Call the police if you need to. But we both know that Jerome ran away because he wanted to, and not because of me.'

'Yes, Larry,' said Stephanie.

As Larry left the bedroom, Stephanie looked down at her phone. Her fingers shaking, she dialled nine-nine-nine, and reported that her son was missing, giving his description. Then she waited a few minutes, until Larry was busy watching television. And that was when she called Ian.

**

When Ian saw that Stephanie was calling him, he picked up the phone at once. He had told her to get in touch if she ever needed anything, but she had only contacted him twice before, and never as early as this.

'What's going on, Steph?' he asked. 'Just filling up my car; give me a minute.'

'Sure,' she said, trying to sound relaxed.

'What's wrong?' asked Ian, as he got back into his car.

'Jerome left this morning,' said Stephanie. 'He's been so unhappy ever since he got sent away from school.'

'Sent home?' Ian asked. 'What for?'

'They say he was skipping class,' said Stephanie. 'And now he's just packed up some things and left. I don't know where he's gone. I just phoned the police; I'm going to see them later. They are doing what they can.'

'Does he have any money?'

'Not much,' said Stephanie. 'He's got some money saved up.' She paused. 'Oh no. He might also have some money from a skills contest he won last year. I know because he gave me half of it. That was about three hundred pounds.'

Ian thought for a second. 'Is his passport still in his room?'

'I'll have a look,' said Stephanie.

'Great,' said Ian. 'I'll just park up at the side of the petrol station. Let me know.'

Stephanie went into Jerome's room and rummaged round for a couple of minutes, and then put her ear to the phone again. 'Thank God,' she said. 'It's still here.'

'So we know he is staying in the UK. That's good, at least.'

'Yes. I suppose.' Stephanie started sobbing. 'I'm sorry, Ian. I'm sorry. I'm just falling to pieces here. I know he's thirteen but he's still my baby.'

'Hey. No need to say sorry, Steph,' said Ian. 'I can't imagine how this feels.'

'I just feel sick,' said Stephanie. She lowered her voice. 'I think he had a big argument last night with Larry, but Larry won't tell me what he said to him. And this morning he just ran off.'

'Larry is still in the flat?' asked Ian.

'Yes.'

'Best not to talk about him right now,' said Ian. 'Just to be safe.'

'You're right, you're right,' said Stephanie. She raised her voice again. 'I'll get in touch with the church and with his school and all his friends. I'm so scared. My stomach is jumping all over the place.'

'Jerome will be fine, he will be fine,' said Ian. 'He is going through a hard time but he isn't wild. I'm sure that wherever he is, he is still trying to be careful. Maybe he just needs some space.'

Stephanie felt a bit better after hearing that. Talking to Ian made her feel calmer.

'You don't sound surprised that he is gone,' she said.

'No,' said Ian. 'I'm not surprised. He has been struggling a little bit. And he hasn't been talking to me. He's been ignoring my calls, my messages. I just wish I had called you before, Steph. Maybe he was going through a much harder time than we all realized.'

'Maybe that school was just too much for him,' said Stephanie. 'My poor baby.'

'Let's not say that just yet,' said Ian. 'I still believe in him.' He went quiet for a while, so long that Stephanie thought he had gone.

'Ian – are you still there?' asked Stephanie.

'Hey, of course, of course,' said Ian. 'I was just thinking of what to do next. Could you put me in touch with your local police station?'

***

That afternoon, after Ian had spoken to the police and to Jerome's school, he posted a short video on his Twitter account. The video showed Ian facing the camera: he looked very sad, and a little bit tired.

So I just want to put this message out there to my friend Jerome Jackson. Jerome, if you see this, if you are listening to this, I just want you to know: we love you. Your mum loves you, your community loves you, I love you. You are a very special young man, and you are going to do wonderful things with your life. To anyone else who is watching this, Jerome went missing from his home in Hackney today. There is a photo of Jerome at the end of this video. If you see him, please buy him a hot chocolate and then please ask him to come home, because we miss him. If you don't mind, it would be great if you could share this video. Please come home, Jerome. It's going to be OK. Lots of love.

***

Jerome sat on a bench at the top of the beach, looking out at the sea. He stretched his feet along the ground, his trainers making small hills out of the pebbles around them. He put his hands into the pockets of his hoodie and pushed them together. He felt safe and comfortable, at last. And, most of all, he felt free.

That morning, he had left his flat and got on the train from Hackney to Highbury and Islington, and then on to King's Cross, and then he had walked to St Pancras and got the train all the way down to Brighton. He had then walked out of the train station and down the hill towards the beach. He wanted to come to Brighton because when he had been there to play football with his church it had made him so happy. The sea was just so slow and still and calm, and he knew that if he came here it would be peaceful.

He looked at his rucksack, which was next to him on the bench. He only had enough clean clothes and enough money to stay away for two days and he didn't know what he was going to do after that. For now, he was just happy staring at the waves coming in and floating away, coming in and floating away for ever.

As Jerome gazed at the waves, a couple walked past in front of him: a man and a woman in their late forties, going for a morning stroll. He raised his head to see that the man was looking straight at him. Jerome quickly lowered his head again, but he could sense that the man was still looking at him.

'Come on, Roland, let's go,' said the woman.

Jerome's heart started to thud twice as fast. Roland had frightened him. He sat there for a few minutes, trying to steady his breathing. He was about to get up and leave when Roland and the woman came back. They were walking more quickly this time.

'Jerome?' asked Roland.

Jerome was so surprised that he knew his name that he stayed sitting where he was.

'We saw Ian's video about you. I follow him on Twitter – I'm a huge Arsenal fan. Anyway. He says that he loves you and he wants you to come home.' He took his phone from his pocket and showed Jerome. 'Look.'

Jerome watched the video and saw the pain in Ian's face. *What a mess I have made*, he thought.

'I can't go home now,' said Jerome. 'I've ruined everything.'

'Not at all,' said Roland. He turned to the woman. 'Marie, has he ruined everything?'

'Of course not,' said Marie. 'Whatever you are going through, you have people who love you. And that means you have won half the battle.'

Roland and Marie sat down either side of Jerome on the bench.

'We can give you a lift back to London,' said Roland. 'Back to the people who love you.'

'It's OK, Jerome. It's OK,' said Marie. She saw that his eyes were growing wet with sadness, and so she put a hand on his shoulder.

Jerome sniffed back his tears. 'But they are going to hate me,' he said.

'They won't,' said Marie. 'Love doesn't work like that. You'll see.' The three of them looked out at the sea, and at the seagulls flying high and free above the waves.

19

MARIE AND ROLAND

As Jerome sat in the back of Marie and Roland's car, counting down the miles towards London, he thought about how he was so scared to go home. He was frightened of Larry, but what worried him most was seeing his mum. He had caused her so much trouble. What if she didn't like him any more?

When Roland had called Jerome's mum to tell her that her son was safe, Jerome had spoken to her on the phone, and he had heard the relief in her voice. But now, as he thought about what she had told him, he was nervous.

'Don't meet me at the flat,' she had said. 'Go to Uncle Ray's. Me and Ian will meet you there this evening.'

Why did she want to do that? Why didn't she want to meet him at the flat? Was she going to be waiting there with all his things packed up in a suitcase, ready to kick him out for ever?

Roland looked into the rear-view mirror and saw Jerome staring down at his hands, clasped tight as if he was about to pray.

'Everything all right back there?' he asked.

'Yes. Yes, I'm fine,' said Jerome.

'It's all right if things aren't fine,' said Roland.

Jerome clasped his hands a little tighter and leaned forward until his seatbelt tugged him back.

'I'm fine,' he said.

'I'm happy to hear that,' said Roland. 'Because you are a lovely young man.'

Jerome saw something splash on his hands – once, twice – and then he realized it was his own tears.

'I'm not fine,' he said. 'I'm not fine at all.' His tears formed a small pool in the gap between his hands. 'Every time I try to do something to feel better, I make it worse,' he said. 'What if I get home and Mum doesn't want me?'

'Oh, Jerome,' said Marie. 'Of course she will want you. You're her baby.'

'We have a daughter,' said Roland. 'Vanessa. She lives all the way in New Zealand with her lovely husband, Laurie. They met when she was travelling through South Asia. Vanessa was always in trouble when she was growing up – and each time she got in trouble, we loved her even more.'

'Remember that time with your book chapter!' said Marie.

'Oh my goodness, yes!' said Roland. 'Jerome, here's a story from when Vanessa was little. So I write books about history. I was working on a long chapter about the Second World War, and I wrote it all out on nice paper. And one day I left the door to my study open, and Vanessa came in, and she dropped all the papers in the bath. She ruined months of work! And she did it just because she liked to see the paper and the ink floating on the water.'

'Oh my goodness,' gasped Jerome.

'The world is a big, scary place sometimes,' said Marie. 'When you are born, it's like you find yourself in the middle of a giant puzzle and no one has given you any of the clues. Even Roland and I still find this world very confusing, and we are old.'

'We are not old!' said Roland.

'Oh, we are very old,' said Marie. 'We are older than black-and-white television.'

Roland howled with laughter.

'Marie Richards,' he said, 'I'm not driving you back to Brighton. You are going to get the train.'

'Not if I keep the car keys,' she said and giggled.

Jerome found himself smiling for the first time that day.

'As I was saying,' said Marie, 'sometimes the world is confusing. And when our children do unusual things, like running away, it's because they are trying to figure out how this world works. And that's all you are doing. Figuring things out.'

'Every child is a gift,' said Roland. 'Vanessa was the naughtiest child in Brighton, and she was just perfect the way she was. And you are a gift too. Your dear mum will be so happy to see you again.'

Jerome unfolded his hands and rubbed them together until they were dry. He leaned back in his seat. The way Roland and Marie joked with each other – that was like the way his mum and dad had been, long before any of this. Some people get to be happy for ever, he thought. Some people only get it for a short time.

'It's going to be OK, Jerome,' said Roland. 'It really is.'

'Thank you so much,' said Jerome. 'I'm fine now,' he said, and he meant it.

***

An hour later, Marie and Roland's car rolled slowly down a quiet street in East London and stopped a few metres away from the barbershop.

'Well, Jerome, it has been a pleasure,' said Marie.

'Absolutely,' said Roland. 'Great job, Marie. And let's swap seats – my turn to drive now.'

'You're not coming inside?' asked Jerome. 'You don't want to meet Ian?'

'No, no,' said Roland. 'That's not why I helped you. We were just trying to do the right thing.'

'Roland, you really should,' said Marie. 'You'll regret it if you don't.'

'No,' said Roland again, and Marie shrugged.

'There's no winning that argument,' she said, and the two of them got out of the car to say goodbye to Jerome. As they walked towards him, he reached out his arms, and then the three of them were hugging in the street. *These people are so kind*, thought Jerome. *People are good, they really are.*

'If I'm ever back in Brighton,' said Jerome, 'is it OK for me to come and see you?'

'Of course you can!' said Marie. 'We will be upset if you don't. Here, let's swap numbers now. And when you come to town, you can stay with us.' She and Roland got back into the car, and Roland started the key in the ignition. Just before he started to drive, he put down his window. He wanted to say one last thing.

'Everybody needs friends, Jerome,' he said. 'Please remember that. You can't go through this life all by yourself. It's just too lonely. If you can, find yourself a best friend. And if you can, find yourself a Marie. And hang on to them.'

Jerome watched their car roll back up the street, around the corner and out of sight. Then he took a long breath, turned, and walked towards the barbershop. It seemed busier in there than usual — there seemed to be a lot of people inside. As soon as he opened the door, he heard a huge cheer. There, in front of him, were several of his friends from his local church.

'Here he is!' exclaimed Reverend Benjamin.

'He was lost, and now he is found!' yelled Manny.

'Oh, Jerome!' said Stephanie. There she was, in the middle of the crowd, her eyes tired but joyful. She looked as if she had not sat down since he went missing. She rushed forward and held him for what seemed like half an hour.

'I didn't think you would come back,' she said. 'Jerome, I love you. Please, please never leave me again.'

'I won't, Mum, I won't,' said Jerome. When they let each other go, Jerome saw Ian standing next to her.

'Ian,' said Jerome, 'I'm so, so sorry. I – I saw all your messages. I just couldn't—'

'Hey, my man,' said Ian. 'We're just so happy that you're home.' He gently rubbed the top of Jerome's head. 'You came to the right place, too! What's this? You really need a haircut.'

'You are right, brother Ian,' said Ray. 'Jerome's hair is looking very bushy up there, I'll sort that out soon. But right now – we must eat!'

It was then that Jerome noticed the amazing smell, and when he looked towards the back of the barbershop, he saw a long table with two trays of food on top of it.

'When we heard you were coming back,' said Ian, 'I ordered some meals from Ijeoma's House. I remembered how much you liked it, so I got enough for you and your friends.'

'Thank you so much,' said Jerome. Then he added: 'You're my friend too, Ian.'

'No,' said Ray, patting Jerome on the head, 'we are your uncles!'

'Come on, you lot,' called Ian to the rest of the room, 'it's been a long day for all of us. Time for dinner!'

As everyone else grabbed a plate and queued up for their food, Jerome shook his head. He couldn't believe all these people had come to see him. But he still couldn't relax.

'What's the matter, Jerome?' asked Ian.

Jerome looked around the room then looked back at Ian.

'It's OK,' said Ian. 'Larry isn't here, and he's not coming.'

Jerome sighed with relief.

'Ah – wait!' said Ian. 'Where are the people who gave you a lift?'

'Roland and Marie,' said Jerome. 'I tried to get them to come in and say hello, but they've already gone back to Brighton.'

'But I wanted to meet them,' said Ian. 'To thank them for bringing you back.'

'Marie was going to come in, but Roland didn't want to get in the way,' said Jerome. 'He's such a big Arsenal fan too. He used to watch you.'

'That's such a shame,' said Ian. He went quiet for a moment, thinking.

'They were so kind to me,' said Jerome.

'You'll see them again, Jerome,' said Ian. 'One rule in life: if you can help it, never let good people leave you.' He put one arm around Jerome's shoulders, and the two of them joined the back of the queue for food.

***

After about an hour had passed, an hour full of good food and conversation, Ian decided it was time to say something. He put down his empty plate and walked up to Jerome, who was leaning against one of the walls, his stomach stuffed full of beef stew. Ian put one of his hands on each of Jerome's shoulders and looked him in the eyes. 'Jerome,' he said. 'Please, as you are standing here, please promise me one thing. Please promise me that you will never, ever run away again.'

'OK,' said Jerome, looking away from Ian.

'Jerome,' said Ian. His voice was quiet and kind and insistent. 'Please, Jerome. That's not good enough. Please look at me, and please promise.'

'I can't,' said Jerome.

'You can't promise?' asked Ian.

'No,' said Jerome. 'I can't look at you. It's just too hard.'

'Jerome, please look at me,' said Ian.

'When I look at you it just reminds me what a mess I have made,' said Jerome. 'And how much I have hurt you and Mum.'

'You haven't hurt us, Jerome,' said Ian. He kept his

hands on Jerome's shoulders, and squeezed them lightly. 'Come on. I know you can do this.'

Jerome looked straight at Ian and took a breath.

'OK,' he said.

'Repeat after me,' said Ian.

'OK.'

'I, Jerome Emanuel Ellington Jackson –'

Jerome burst out laughing.

'Oh my gosh. I can't believe you know my middle names. Who told you them?'

Ian grinned and put his fingers to his lips, his smile saying, *I'm not telling you, there is no way in the world I'm telling you.*

'Mum told you, right?' asked Jerome. 'Oh my gosh. I'm so going to get her back for this.' Jerome shook his head. 'Amazing. OK.' He wiped the tears of laughter from his eyes and took another breath. He was much more relaxed now. 'I, Jerome Emanuel Ellington Jackson…' he said.

'… Promise that I'll never, ever even consider running away from home again,' said Ian.

'… Promise that I'll never, ever even consider running away from home again.'

'I promise,' said Ian, 'that I'll always call on my community when I need them.'

'I promise,' repeated Jerome, 'that I'll always call on my community when I need them.'

'And I promise,' said Ian, 'that when I'm running through on goal in the final minute, I'll remain calm…'

'That when I'm running through on goal in the final minute, I'll remain calm…'

'That when the goalkeeper approaches, I shall dance around him…'

'That when the goalkeeper approaches, I shall dance around him…'

'… Or float the ball over his head, as slowly as a cloud crosses the ocean.'

Jerome burst out laughing.

'Don't laugh!' said Ian, but he was laughing too. 'Say it with me, everyone!' He turned to everyone, and they yelled:

'Or float the ball over his head, as slowly as a cloud crosses the ocean!'

'Here ends the lesson,' said Ian. 'Can I get an amen?' he asked.

'AMEN!' shouted the crowd. 'AMEN!'

Jerome shook his head, his heart full of joy. *These are my people,* he thought. *My people. I can never leave them again.*

20

STILL GOT IT

The next day, it felt as if Jerome's mum was on the phone all the time. Now that Jerome had returned, Stephanie had to see if his school wanted to take him back, and so she had several phone calls with his teachers. Jerome sat in his room and listened as she walked up and down the living room, talking loudly to each of them as she got more stressed.

Not everyone at St Joseph's was sure that they were ready to welcome Jerome. His coach could not wait for him to train with the team again, but his housemaster was less keen. 'Mrs Jackson,' he told her, 'we have many rules at St Joseph's, and I'm not sure if Jerome is ready to obey them yet.'

Jerome was nervous now. What if they kicked him out of school? What if he had ruined his big chance? He went to the kitchen to get a glass of water and as he walked through the doorway, he saw Larry standing there, leaning against the counter with his hands folded in front of his chest. He looked like he had been waiting for him. Jerome started to feel sick.

'So you thought you could come out of hiding and everything would go back to normal,' said Larry.

Jerome tried to talk but his tongue felt as if it was glued to the bottom of his mouth.

'Ah, so you did,' continued Larry. 'What you need to understand is that in the real world you can't just run away from your problems. They catch up with you.' He unfolded his arms and put his hands down by his sides, resting them on the counter behind him. 'Just like they caught up with Aaron, and now he's been locked up. You got away just in time. But next time you won't be so lucky. And then mummy's little golden boy will be locked up too.'

'But that wasn't my fault!' said Jerome.

'Tell that to the police,' said Larry. 'You're losing it, Jerome. First you get sent home from school, then you run away. Face it. You are going to break. The only question is when.'

'Good news, Jerome!' said Stephanie, walking into the kitchen, looking tired but happy. But when she saw Larry standing there the joy fled from her face.

'What's happening here?' she asked. Jerome looked at the floor and said nothing.

'Nothing,' said Larry. 'Just welcoming him home.' He pushed himself forward off the counter and strolled out of the kitchen. 'I'm off to have a lie down now. Enjoy your good news, Jerome, whatever it is.'

Stephanie watched him walk into the bedroom, and then she shut the kitchen door behind her. As soon as she did, the flush of happiness returned to her cheeks.

'So,' she said, 'I was having a little bit of trouble with your school, and then Ian gave them a call, and now everything is OK. They say you can go back next week.'

Jerome looked down at his hands and realized that he had been crossing his fingers all the time.

'Another chance,' he said. 'Mum, that's all I wanted.'

'They say it's your last chance,' said Stephanie. 'They say you just need to calm down and not let everything go to your head. No making up your own tactics just because you think you are smarter than Mr Baxter. And Ian said that he was going to help with your training.'

'Wow! Wow! Mum, Ian is going to come to school and train us?'

'No,' said Stephanie. 'He is going to train you. Just you. You're going to do all your football training as normal and then he is going to spend more time with you too. He is going to start tomorrow morning and then give you a couple more sessions this season.'

'Yes! Yes! Yes!' yelled Jerome. He was so happy that he felt as if he had scored a goal, and he nearly put his hand in the air to celebrate.

'Calm down,' said Stephanie. 'Jerome, it's not going to be easy when you go back to school. They will be watching you for any bad behaviour. No more missing classes, OK?'

'No more,' said Jerome.

'Good,' said Stephanie. 'Ian will be here tomorrow morning to pick you up for training. So make sure you get plenty of sleep.'

'Yes, Mum!' said Jerome. 'I can't wait!'

***

Jerome heard a tap on his bedroom window and sat up at once, rubbing his eyes in alarm. It was still so early. Who was trying to wake him up in the middle of the night? He pulled back the curtain, and as soon as Ian saw him, he winked.

'Your mum told me to come and knock for you. Ready to go?' he asked Jerome through the open window.

'Yes – yes,' said Jerome, 'I'm wide awake.'

'Of course you are,' said Ian. 'I'll be waiting out here.'

Jerome stumbled across the room, stuffed himself into a tracksuit, grabbed his boots then went out into the walkway outside his flat. Ian was already standing downstairs next to his car, holding a pair of his own boots and a brand-new football. 'Today's tools,' he said. 'Let's get to work.'

Jerome climbed into Ian's car and they drove down to Hackney Marshes. It was still so early when they got there that the mist swirled around their ankles. They jogged to one of the pitches at the corner of the field, where a young man in goalkeeping kit was leaning against one of the goalposts. When he saw them, he stood upright and shivered, rubbing his hands together.

'Pleased to meet you, Jerome,' said the keeper, offering his hand. Jerome shook it quickly, and gladly.

'This is Seb,' said Ian. 'He is doing very well at Crystal Palace. Every so often, when I need some help with a junior player, he joins me for some shooting practice.'

'Let's do it,' said Seb. 'What are we doing today?'

'The whole lot,' said Ian. 'One-on-ones, shooting from distance, chips, volleys, you name it.'

Seb smiled. 'The usual then,' he said, jogging to his goal-line. 'Come on, Jay-Jay. Let's see what you've got.'

'How do you know I'm called Jay-Jay?' asked Jerome, smiling.

'Because top goalkeepers do their homework,' said Seb. 'And I've studied how you play. So let's go for it.'

And Jerome went for it. He used every skill he had. He hit the ball with his left foot, his right, hit it hard, hit it with swerve. And nothing worked. Nothing at all. He shot and shot and shot for thirty-four minutes and he didn't score. Seb was amazing. He was even better than Billy Seymour. He could save the ball with anything – his hands, his knees, his feet. As Jerome fetched the ball and tried and again and again, Ian watched from the side of the pitch and didn't say anything. At last he spoke.

'Right, let's stop for a break,' he said. He went to his car and took out two bottles of water, throwing one of them to Seb and one to Jerome. 'Great job, Seb,' he said. Then he turned to Jerome. 'Well done,' he said. 'Very well done.'

Jerome was confused.

'Oh, thanks, Ian,' he said. 'I don't feel like I did well at all. I didn't score a single goal.'

'That's not what I was testing you for,' said Ian. 'I was testing you to see if you would give up. And you never, ever did. You didn't complain once. I was watching the way you held your head, your shoulders. And you were disappointed, but you didn't stop thinking of new ideas. Each time you didn't score, you kept trying; you kept going. And the best strikers aren't the most skilful ones. They are the ones who never give up.'

'Oh,' said Jerome.

'Yes,' said Ian. 'You can be one of the very best. And now we need to make it easier for you to score. Are you ready?'

Jerome nodded. He was definitely ready. He hadn't come all the way to this freezing cold pitch at this time of morning for nothing.

'So here is some advice,' said Ian. 'Every time the goalkeeper looks at you, he is looking for clues. He is trying to work out where you are going to kick the ball before you even kick it. So your job is to stop giving him clues. You need to be a mystery that he can't solve.'

Ian stood opposite Jerome. 'Right now, when you kick the ball, your body is telling Seb everything. When you put up your right hand like that, he knows you are going to kick it left. The moment you put down your head, he knows you are getting ready to shoot. So you need to stop doing that. If you can keep your head up when you kick it, then you can see which way the goalkeeper is going to jump. That way, you can see all of his clues.'

Jerome nodded, and then he thought for a bit. *This is exactly what Toby was telling me,* he thought. He didn't want to complain but this sounded hard. Really hard. Ian was telling him to kick the ball without looking at it! That was like trying to climb out of a swimming pool without touching the sides!

Ian smiled. He could tell what Jerome was thinking.

'I know it sounds difficult,' he said, 'but I'm only asking you because most footballers are not good enough to do it. And you are. Try it.'

Jerome placed the ball five metres in front of him. He stared at it so that he could remember exactly where it was, and then he ran towards it. At the last minute he looked up and swung his left foot at it – and his left foot swung through the empty air and his right foot tumbled underneath him. He fell flat on his bottom.

'Not bad for a first try,' said Ian. 'Again.'

Jerome tried again. This time he didn't fall over but he missed the ball by half a metre.

'Better,' said Ian. 'Again.'

This time Jerome made contact with the ball, but the shot was weak and it rolled into Seb's hands.

'That's more like it,' said Ian. 'Now try it with more power.' Jerome stepped back five metres. Before he started to run towards the ball, Ian said:

'Jay-Jay. You've got this.'

He's right, thought Jerome. *He's right.*

He stepped back, and ran forward, watching the ball then at the last minute watching Seb. He swung his left leg towards the ball and, as Seb dived low to his right, the ball tore into the bottom left-hand corner of the net!

'Goaaaaaaalll!' shouted Ian. 'Oh my goodness, Jerome Jackson with the no-look penalty! The crowd is going absolutely wild!'

Seb rose to his knees and clapped. 'That's brilliant, Jerome!' he said. 'So so good. I didn't know where you were going to put it!'

'My man,' said Ian. 'You know what, Jerome? You keep working hard, you will keep surprising yourself!'

Jerome wanted to speak but he was too busy smiling. He had only scored one goal in forty minutes, but he felt like he had just won the World Cup!

'One last lesson for today, Jerome,' said Ian. 'One last thing. I have been told one thing by your coach. He says you have all the skill but sometimes you get a bit worried when you are running towards the goal, all by yourself. He says that sometimes you could be a bit calmer.'

'Yeah, that's true,' said Jerome. He thought back to a

good chance he had missed against Serpentine, a school from West London. 'I find it a bit hard to relax.'

'That's fine,' said Ian. 'I think I have an idea.' He went back to his car, and he took out his smartphone and a pair of headphones. 'Here, put these on.'

Jerome put them on and listened. It was piano music, long and slow. Listening to it, Jerome felt as if he was walking through a quiet town on a Sunday afternoon; a town where dogs were lying asleep on sunny street corners and where couples were walking arm-in-arm after church. As the music poured in through his ears, rushing through every anxious corner of his mind, Jerome found that it made him feel peaceful.

'Wow,' he said.

'Yes,' said Ian. 'That's music by a man called Erik Satie. It's almost 150 years old, but it sounds even older. When you are running towards goal, all by yourself, I want you to think of this music. Imagine that Erik Satie is playing piano in your head. I think it will calm you down.'

'I'll try that, definitely,' said Jerome.

'Good man,' said Ian. 'Now, let's practise a few more shots before we go home.' He put the ball down on the edge of the area, and walked back five metres, ready to walk forward and shoot. 'Come on, Seb,' he called. 'Let's see if I've still got it.' As Ian jogged forward, he was suddenly thirty years younger, and the empty park became a set of stands bursting with singing supporters. Ian struck the ball with his right foot and it surged off to the right as if it was going wide of the goal and then it swerved back at the last moment, just as Seb stood there watching it. It struck the inside edge of the right-hand post, *ting*, and soared into the top right-hand corner of the net.

Ian turned back towards Jerome and did his famous celebration, the one he had done so many times at Highbury: he raised the forefinger of his left hand high in the air, then dropped his left hand back to his side and then made the same movement with his right hand. 'What do you think, Jerome?' he asked. 'Has this uncle still got it?'

'Yes, Uncle,' agreed Jerome. 'Still got it!'

YOU CAN'T STOP ME ANY MORE

Jerome went back to St Joseph's the following week, and for the next two weeks he worked harder than ever. After finishing class each day, he went to his room and read over his notes for an hour before dinner. After football training was finished, he went to his coaches and asked them what he could do better the next time they trained.

So many people were happy with Jerome. Mr Franklin called Stephanie one evening to say how delighted he was with Jerome's classwork. 'Your boy has been exceptional since he returned to us,' he said. Toby couldn't believe how much better Jerome was in training. And Mr Baxter sent Ian a long voice note about all the brilliant goals that Jerome was scoring during practice. 'If he can do this in our big games, he is going to be incredible,' said Mr

Baxter. 'Jerome was very good when he first came to us, but ever since he got back to school, he is playing at a different level. His finishing is so much better. More calm, more precise. I don't know what you said to him, Wrighty, but he's been listening to you. Let's hope he can keep it up.'

But not everyone was happy with Jerome. One of those people was Gavin Bradley. After Jerome ran away, Gavin thought that St Joseph's were going to kick Jerome out of school and that he would never see him again. So when he saw Jerome turn up to football training and play better than ever, he didn't like it. He got very angry but he didn't say anything at first. But one day after football training, as Jerome walked back to his house, Gavin and two of his friends followed him.

'Hey, you,' said Gavin.

Jerome looked over his shoulder and saw Gavin standing there, with Stanley and Eugene standing either side of him like dogs guarding a house.

'You know my name,' said Jerome, and he kept walking.

'So now you are back at school like everything is forgiven,' said Gavin. 'But we don't forgive you. You ran away from the team when we needed you.'

'Nice try,' said Jerome.

'We joke about what happened to you all the time,' said Gavin. 'Getting kicked out of our hot tub. We even have a name for you—'

'Gavin,' said Jerome, turning round and walking straight

for him, stopping just a metre away. 'You and me and Stanley and Eugene are all very good at football. So let's just play football. Let's win something this season. And I'm not interested in your nicknames. I was talking to Ian one day and he said they used to call him everything. The worst names you could imagine. And he told me there are just some people on this earth who hate people who look like us and that's just their problem and not ours. So you can call me what you like and you can do what you like but I have too many people who care about me. You hurt me and we both know that, but you can't stop me any more. See you tomorrow.'

Jerome turned around and began to walk away. Gavin opened his mouth to speak, and Eugene and Stanley looked at him, ready to cheer on whatever he said, but Gavin closed his mouth again, and put his hands on his hips, and just stood there until Jerome was out of sight.

***

There was one other person who was not happy that Jerome was doing well in school, and that was Larry. Each time he heard another story from Stephanie about Jerome's success, he got more upset. And one evening, as he and Stephanie were watching television together, Larry lost his temper.

They sat together on the sofa, with Stephanie resting her head on his lap, waiting for the start of *Strange Nature*, Stephanie's favourite show. Each week, the presenter would discuss a different animal, and all the weird and wonderful things that made it special. That week, they were going to talk about the snowy owl. Just before *Strange Nature* was about to start, there was an advert for an upcoming football match, a Champions League game between Benfica and Juventus.

'Look at that,' said Stephanie. 'The way Jerome is going, he will be playing in that match one day.'

'Jerome, Jerome, Jerome,' said Larry. 'It's like you don't know any other words.'

'Larry!' Stephanie looked up at him.

'You are spoiling that boy,' said Larry. 'He just has to sulk a little bit and he gets everything he wants.'

'I'm not spoiling him,' said Stephanie. 'And he is not "that boy". He is my son.'

'He goes to a fancy school, and he has a famous footballer friend,' said Larry. 'Sounds like he's spoiled to me.'

'Sounds like you're jealous,' said Stephanie.

'Get your head off me!' shouted Larry. Stephanie sat straight up as he jumped to his feet and stood over her. Her eyes were wide and full of fear.

'All week I work and pay what I can to help you in this house,' he said, 'and I never hear, "thank you, Larry." I never hear it from him, and I never hear it from you.'

'Larry, please sit down,' said Stephanie. 'Please, there is such a nice programme coming on. Please, let's just watch that together.'

'No,' said Larry. 'You call me jealous of Jerome. But it's like you are making us compete against each other. Every time I want to spend time with you, Jerome gets in the way. Everything is about him, and what he needs. But what about what I need?'

'Oh, Larry, but this is silly—'

Larry raised his right foot and brought it down on the middle of the coffee table, smashing straight through the glass. A cloud of frightened crystals leapt into the air, then scattered everywhere across the floor.

'That's silly, is it?' asked Larry, as Stephanie scrambled to the far corner of the sofa, away from him. He picked up the coffee table by two of its legs and swung it with all his strength against the wall, breaking it in half. 'Is this silly?'

'Larry, you're scaring me!' said Stephanie.

'Rubbish!' said Larry. 'You're enjoying this!'

'I'm not!' said Stephanie. 'Larry, I promise I'm not!' As she looked up at him, tears fled down her cheeks.

'You're *loving* it!' said Larry. 'You know just what to say so that you can make me blow up like a bomb! Oh, let's call Larry jealous and see what he does next! Well, now the bomb has exploded, Stephanie! So what are you going to do about it?'

Stephanie felt as if she could not breathe, as if her lungs were suddenly full of dust. She waved her hands in front of her mouth, as if she was trying to push air down her throat. She had to get out of there, she had to.

'I need to go for a walk,' she said. 'I just need to walk around the block.' She stood up and as she was about to leave the living room Larry grabbed her wrist and held it, staring her in the eye.

'Running away, just like your son,' he said. 'Maybe it is just what your family does.'

Stephanie went to the hallway and put on her coat and trainers and then walked slowly out of the door. Larry followed her out of the flat and stood on the balcony to watch her. Stephanie kept walking slowly until she got round the corner of the apartment block and then she ran, ran as fast as she could, all the way to Hackney Central and jumped on the train to Haggerston. Then ran from the train to the front door of her friend Amy's flat and when Amy opened the door Stephanie fell into her arms and just started sobbing, sobbing, and didn't stop for twenty minutes. Amy just held her. When Stephanie was finished, Amy looked down at her poor, lovely, sad, tired friend and she asked, 'Larry?' Stephanie nodded, and Amy said, 'I love you Stephanie Jackson. You are safe, and you can stay here as long as you like.'

**

Stephanie woke up the next morning and when she saw what time it was she almost fell out of bed in shock.

'Oh my goodness,' said Stephanie, pulling on her clothes and running into the corridor. 'I'm hours late for work! They're going to sack me!'

'Not to worry, angel,' said Amy. 'I called them and told them you were feeling sick. They know you've been having a tough time with Jerome. They completely understand.' She opened the kitchen door and a delicious smell floated out. 'Come on, I've made pancakes. Thought you might like some.'

***

Half an hour later, Stephanie sat back in her chair, absolutely full. 'Oh my goodness,' she said. 'Amy, I badly needed that.'

'I could tell,' said Amy, laughing. 'You ate those pancakes like they were the last ones on earth!'

'I did,' said Stephanie, slowly rubbing her belly. 'I am going to need a lie down after that.'

'Be my guest,' said Amy. 'I'll make sure to be quiet, so I don't disturb you.'

'Thanks so much, Amy,' said Stephanie. 'Before I do, do you mind if I borrow your phone to call someone? I don't want to turn on my phone just yet. I know it will be full of messages from Larry.'

'Of course you can,' said Amy. She paused. 'Stephanie,' she said, 'you know you don't have to go back to your flat tonight.'

Stephanie silently held open her hand for the phone, and Amy gently placed it into her palm. 'I'll just be in the living room,' said Amy, 'I'll let you have some privacy to talk.' She stood up, gave Stephanie a quick kiss on the forehead, and walked out of the kitchen and down the hallway.

Stephanie took a notebook from her pocket and opened it. This was where she kept Ian's number – she didn't want Larry to find it. As she dialled she realized that her hands were still shaking a little – she was still frightened from last night. After seven rings, Ian answered.

'Hello?' He sounded unsure.

'Hi Ian! Hi, it's me, Stephanie. Jerome's mum.'

'Hey Stephanie! How's it going? You caught me at a good time – I'm just up in Manchester, finishing off some TV work. Sorry I didn't answer at once – I didn't recognize the number.'

'Oh sorry, that's my fault! I should have sent you a text. I just… I couldn't call from my phone.'

'Stephanie, what's the matter?'

Stephanie didn't speak for a few seconds. Ian listened, patiently. Finally, she spoke.

'Larry got really bad last night,' she said. 'Worse than before.'

'Oh, Steph,' said Ian. 'I am so sorry. Where are you? Are you okay?'

'I'm at my friend Amy's place,' said Stephanie. 'I stayed here last night. I just couldn't be in the same place as him. I didn't even take my toothbrush.'

'I wish I was in London today', said Ian. 'I would have driven straight over.'

'Hey, no, it's fine,' said Stephanie. 'I just wanted to talk to you about it, to let you know.'

'Thanks so much. Does Jerome know?'

'I can't tell him, not yet. He is doing so well in school. I don't want to upset him.'

'I understand that. How are you feeling?'

'I don't know,' said Stephanie. 'I just don't know. It's like there is a Good Larry and a Bad Larry. And we are having a nice quiet time and then suddenly the Bad Larry comes out. Like last night. It was all fine and then I said how well Jerome was doing and he just exploded. He kept shouting in my face, and he started breaking things. It felt like he was out of control. And he was never like that before.'

'Oh, Steph,' said Ian. 'It just sounds like he is getting worse and worse, you know? If you need, you and Jerome can come and stay at mine for a bit. Just to get you right away from all of that.'

'Thank you so much,' said Stephanie. 'We will do that if we need to, we will. I will go back tonight once he has had a chance to cool down, and I will just see how the next couple of weeks go. To be fair to Larry, he has been having a tough time with shifts at work, he has been a bit stressed. Maybe things will just calm down a bit.'

'I hope you're right,' said Ian. 'My mum always hoped my stepdad would calm down, but he never did. I have never met Larry, but he sounds like such an angry man. And I worry that the anger is just too much for him, and for all of you.'

'I worry too, Ian. I worry so much. Just when Jerome is getting settled, I don't want to take him out of the only home he has ever known.'

'I understand,' said Ian. 'But if it ever gets too much, please will you let me know?'

'I will, I promise.'

'Will be thinking of you and Jerome and praying for you. Lots of love.'

'Lots of love.'

22

STILL SCARED

When she got back to her own flat that night she was still scared. But when she opened the front door and walked through into the living room, she had never seen and smelled the place so clean.

'I thought I would tidy it up a bit,' said Larry. He was sitting on the sofa wearing a new shirt and a smart pair of trousers. In front of him was a brand-new coffee table. 'About time we got rid of the old one,' he joked. 'I was going to cook something, but I don't have that much skill in the kitchen. I was thinking we could go to dinner in Haggerston. Get ready in half an hour?'

Stephanie was tired but she was so relieved to see Larry in a better mood that she agreed. She put on a nice blue dress and they had a lovely meal at the Turkish barbecue grill, and after dinner they walked along the canal. And Larry never asked where she went when she left him last night, and he told so many funny jokes, and he looked just as handsome as the first day she met him. They walked home hand in hand, and Larry talked about how proud he was of Jerome, and how he was sure that Jerome's dad would be proud too. When they got back to the flat the silver moon hung high over their heads, shining softly and gracefully, as if it was welcoming them home.

'Larry,' said Stephanie, 'tonight was just perfect. Thank you.'

'No, thank you,' said Larry.

'And last night,' said Stephanie, 'last night...'

'Was a mistake,' said Larry. 'And it will never happen again.'

'Never?' asked Stephanie.

'Never.'

***

The next two weeks were as happy as Larry and Stephanie had been in years. There were no arguments at all, and they spent so much time laughing with each other. Some nights, when Stephanie came home from work, Larry would meet her at the door and dance with her in the hallway, their favourite music playing in the background. Another time, he even cooked for her. Meanwhile, Jerome was enjoying school so much that he didn't even come home at the weekend, because he was too busy working on his studies and his football. Whenever he called his mum, she sounded so relaxed, like she wasn't worrying any more.

For the first time in a long time, Jerome felt as if things might really end up just fine.

And then, one Sunday morning, he went home.

That Sunday felt different. It felt different because, when Jerome walked towards the flat, he didn't feel afraid of seeing Larry. He was even looking forward to seeing him, because his mum was saying so many nice things about him. And he had so much good news to share. His team had got to the semi-final of the UK Schools Cup and he had a good chance of being in the starting eleven. And he had even come second in his class in a biology test, and fourth in maths. It was all happening for him, it really was.

It was just past eleven in the morning when he got back to the flat. As he turned the key in the lock, he heard the television in the background, but when he walked into the living room it was empty. *Maybe Mum and Larry left it on last night by accident*, he thought. Something else was strange. The coffee table was different. He turned the television off and turned to walk back to his bedroom. And suddenly Larry was standing right over him, like a huge oak tree that was getting ready to fall.

Jerome gasped. Larry had never been so close to him. His nose was just a few centimetres from Jerome's forehead and his breath smelled like the inside of a dustbin. Larry stayed there for a while, ten seconds, twenty, and then he stepped back two paces and stared Jerome straight in the eye. His eyes were two angry suns, burning large and yellow.

'Here he is,' said Larry. 'Jerome Jackson, the champion.'

Jerome smiled, but it was not a happy smile. It was how you smile when you are a small forest animal who has just stepped on a branch and woken up a hungry wolf.

'Hello, Larry,' said Jerome.

'Champion Jerome,' said Larry. 'Everybody loves him. Doesn't matter how much he messes up. There is always someone to clean up after him.'

'I'm sorry, Larry,' said Jerome. 'I don't want to make you angry.'

Larry's eyes were too bright, too scary. Jerome couldn't look at them so he looked at the ground.

'You should be sorry,' said Larry. 'Your mum is so happy when she is just with me and when you come back home everything changes. She is so tired from looking after you. Having a hard job and a young boy who is always in trouble is too much for her.'

'I don't want to be in your way, Larry,' said Jerome. He already wished he had stayed in school, that he had never come home. He tried to walk past Larry, but Larry kept moving from side to side, to block his way. 'Please, Larry. I just want to get to my room. I'll just get some food from the shops and then I'll go in my room and be very quiet, I won't annoy you. You won't even know I'm there. And then I'll go straight back to school tonight.'

'Oh, very clever of you,' said Larry. 'You're going to run away from Larry like he's the big bad wolf.'

'No, I didn't mean that,' said Jerome.

'What did you mean then? What did you mean?' Larry roared and opened his mouth so wide that it looked as if he was preparing to eat Jerome.

Jerome felt desperate. He stepped to his left, Larry followed him, and then sharply to his right, as if he was trying to dribble past a defender. As Larry stumbled, Jerome sprinted past him and into his bedroom, slamming the door shut behind him, locking it and stuffing his bed against it. As soon as he did that, Larry began hammering on the door with his hands.

'Let me in there or I will break the door down!' howled Larry. 'Let me in there!'

Crack!

Crack!

Larry was kicking the door! Jerome could hear him stepping back and then leaping against the door with two feet. Jerome's bed shuddered with the force of Larry's attack and some of his books fell from his desk to the floor.

'Larry! What are you doing?' cried Stephanie. Larry had woken her up and Jerome could hear her feet shuffling anxiously down the corridor towards his room. But that didn't stop Larry. It just made him worse.

'You want to behave like a wild animal?' barked Larry.

'I will show you a wild animal. You let me in there!'

Crack!

Crack!

Flakes of paint flew from the door. Jerome shoved his hands in his pockets for his phone, but his hands were shaking so much that when he took his phone out he dropped it, and it bounced under his bed and out of sight. *Oh no!* He dropped to his hands and knees and scrambled for the phone in the dark. Under the gap in the door he saw Larry's boots jumping up and down. He saw Stephanie's slippers and he heard her sobbing. She was talking to Larry now; Jerome couldn't hear what they were saying but it sounded like she was trying to calm him down. Jerome started crying too. Why was Larry always so angry?

There was his phone! He grabbed it and sat up and, blinking away his tears, he managed to find Ian's number. He dialled and Ian picked up the phone at once. Just then, Larry started kicking again. *Crack! Crack!*

'What did we do wrong, Ian?' asked Jerome. 'What did we do to deserve this?'

'Jerome ,what's happening there? Is it Larry?'

'Yes,' said Jerome, 'He's trying to kick in my door! I didn't even do anything, I just came home, and I ran into my room and he ran after me, and now he is trying to break in!'

'Jerome, you have to call the police!'

'But—'

'Jerome! Please! You have to call the police! This is not some argument you can handle. What Larry is doing is so, so wrong. Please, hang up the phone right now. I am going to call the police even if you won't. And I am going to call you back as soon as I have called them!'

Ian hung up and Jerome stared at the phone in his hand and then he began to dial *nine, nine, nine* –

'Operator.'

'Hello, hello this is Jerome Jackson, I live at number 49 David Emmanuel Estate, in Hackney. I am just, I am just in my bedroom and my mum's boyfriend is trying to break into my room. I'm scared and my mum is in the corridor screaming. He's been bad before but never like this, please send someone, just listen to him! His name is Larry Reynolds, I'm so scared, please send someone, number 49, David Emmanuel Estate, Hackney, please, please!

'Mr Jackson—'

'Please, please just send someone, I don't know how long he needs, Larry Reynolds, my bed is against the door—'

Jerome hung up and his phone rang at once, it was Ian, and he answered, 'Ian, I did it, I did it!'

'Good boy, Jerome, I called them too. They're sending someone, they're coming at once. You just hang in there, I called your mum and told her to get in her bedroom and lock the door. She's on the phone with my wife now, my wife is talking to her and making sure she is calm. The police are coming to help you. Don't worry Jerome, don't worry. Just stay on the phone with me.'

'Yes, Ian!'

The top of the door bulged forward and some of the wood sounded like it was snapping – and then the sirens came, so many of them, wailing from far away and then arriving at the foot of their block of flats. Then came the sounds of boots, the police clattering up the stairs, along the hallway and up to the front door of the flat. But Larry didn't stop kicking, so they yelled and broke through the front door, and then Larry stopped kicking. He shouted at the police and then there was the sound of shoving and struggling in the corridor, and he kept shouting but then his voice got quieter and quieter, and the boots moved away.

'Jerome?' said Ian.

'It's so quiet now,' said Jerome. 'It sounded like there were so many people and now there's none. I think they're taking him away. Thank you so much, Ian.'

'Hey, I know how it feels, Jerome. I know the fear. You feel it all over your body. Like you're having a fever.'

'You really know,' said Jerome.

'I do,' said Ian. 'I do. Look, you can just stay in your room for now. The fear will be gone. You don't have to see him.'

But Jerome wanted to see Larry. 'Ian,' he said, 'I will call you later, I have to go.'

He hung up and all of a sudden he was pulling his

bed back from his door and then running outside to the balcony. He looked down and six police cars were driving away, and somewhere in one of them was Larry. Jerome ran back into the flat and his mum was standing there in her dressing gown and slippers. Her face looked like so sad and so tired.

'Maybe he was always just Bad Larry,' she said. 'I am so sorry Jerome, I am so sorry.'

And Jerome said, 'No, no, no, Mum, don't say sorry,' and they wrapped each other up as tightly as they could in each other's' arms.

'Please don't be sad, Mum,' Jerome said. 'I love you so much, Mum. It's over, it's over, it's over.'

23

'LET'S GO, ST JOE'S!'

Now that Larry had been taken away, Jerome hoped that everything would get back to normal. It did, but not at first. For the next week he was too scared to sleep with the light off. He was also worried about his mum being at home by herself. He only relaxed when the police told his mother that, whatever happened from now, Larry was not coming back to live with them.

Jerome knew that he had to be calm, because the biggest game of the season was coming up. In two days' time, St Joseph's were going to play against Kingsview, last year's national champions, in the semi-finals of the UK Schools Cup. There would be some big clubs watching him and this was his chance to show what he could do.

But, when Jerome saw the team to play against

Kingsview, he did not feel calm. He felt sick, and then sad. He was going to be a substitute again. He went to see his coach to ask what he had been doing wrong, because he thought he had been playing well.

'You haven't done anything wrong,' said Mr Baxter. 'It's just that we have a different tactical plan for today. But you will get your chance, you will. When it comes to the closing part of the game, we will need you.'

After speaking with Mr Baxter, Jerome was still upset, and so he called Ian.

'Jerome! How you doing?'

'Not so good,' said Jerome. 'They've put me on the bench for Saturday's game. I just feel like such a loser.'

'This is a big chance for you, Jerome,' said Ian.

'It doesn't feel like one.'

'I know. But I started one of the best games of my life on the bench,' said Ian. 'It was maybe the game that changed my life.'

'The FA Cup Final? 1990, against Manchester United?'

'Yes, you've watched it?'

'Of course I have! I was studying it last week. You came on – twenty minutes to go.'

'Twenty-one.'

'OK, twenty-one!' said Jerome, laughing.

'Trust me, Jerome, I remember it so well. I was counting down every second! Couldn't wait to get on. I was so desperate to get out there. But I knew I would score. I just knew.'

'And you did! Twice!'

'I did! And you can do that too.'

'But Ian,' said Jerome. 'I'm not Ian Wright.'

'You're not,' said Ian. 'You're better.'

'No,' said Jerome. 'Who am *I*?'

'You are one of the bravest people I have ever met,' said Ian. 'You have had so many setbacks, but you just keep trying. Look how brave you were to call the police on Larry. And look at you now. Playing for one of the best schools in the country. Amazing.'

'I never saw it like that,' said Jerome.

'You don't,' said Ian. 'But you should. I have known you for just a few months, but what I can't believe is that you never ask me for anything. I have sons who play professional football. I'm friends with some of the best footballers who ever played. But you never ask for anything – no introductions to footballers, no autographs, nothing. You just want to do it your own way.'

'But I don't ask for anything because I just see you as my friend,' said Jerome.

'I know,' said Ian. 'But you don't have to do everything alone, Jerome. Not any more.'

'Thank you, Ian.' Jerome felt his eyelids heating up and thought he was going to cry.

'We're here for you,' said Ian. 'All of us. We're going to come and watch you on Saturday, the whole family. And your coach is going to ask you to come on and change everything and when they ask you, you will have to be ready. And you know what, Jerome? I trust you. I know you will be ready.'

'Ian, thank you so much.' Jerome looked down at his feet and he saw his tears splashing off his trainers. 'I'll be ready.'

'Love you, Jerome.'

'Love you too.'

***

On the day of the semi-final, the weather was perfect. There were only two small clouds in the sky, the rest of which was an endless bright blue. And the home crowd was so loud. As Jerome got changed with his teammates, he could hear them chanting all the way from the dressing room. As St Joseph's jogged on to the pitch, the crowd roared as if they had scored a goal. Jerome had never seen so many of them – it felt as if the whole school was watching them, all the teachers and students and some of their friends, and lots of girls from Queen Elizabeth's. And there, by one of the corner flags, wearing a green-and-gold St Joseph's scarf, was Ian. And was that one of his sons who used to play for Arsenal? And was that his daughter, and his wife? Jerome waved at Ian, and Ian waved back.

'Jerome!' said Gavin. 'Keep your mind on the game!'

'I have never been more ready,' said Jerome. 'I'm just taking all this in.'

And then the crowd stopped roaring.

A small gap formed in the middle of the crowd, and through that narrow corridor jogged a group of some of the biggest schoolboys Jerome had ever seen. Kingsview were huge. Standing there in their all-white kits, they looked like a team of polar bears. Some of them even had beards. As they walked to their half, they smiled and laughed. They knew everyone was scared of them.

One of them pointed at Jerome. 'Heard about you,' he said. 'We've got a plan for you.' Then he walked away. Jerome looked at Gavin, who looked worried: now he was thinking too much about the game. But Jerome wasn't afraid at all.

Kingsview won the toss and decided to kick off. Their striker passed it to one of their central midfielders, then to one of their centre backs, then their left back, then their right wing, then onwards. St Joseph's just could not get the ball. One minute went past, then two minutes. The crowd was quiet before, but now it was silent. It took almost three minutes into the game for a St Joseph's player to touch the ball – when Toby slid in to tackle their left wing – and when he did that, there was an enormous yell from the corner of the pitch. Everyone looked over and there was Ian and his family, who were waving their St Joseph's scarves above their heads.

'Let's go, St Joe's!' cried Ian. The crowd roared, and after a few seconds they started chanting again.

But St Joseph's still struggled. Kingsview weren't just big and skilful, they were fast. Really fast. Every time a

St Joseph's player got the ball, three or four Kingsview players surrounded him, like a fog. The only reason that the score was still 0–0 at half-time was because Billy Seymour was having the game of his life. He made six saves in total: two of them were very good, and four of them were incredible. The last save was so good that the striker was already celebrating; he thought he had scored with a header, only for Billy to leap all the way across his goal and flick it over the bar with the top of his hand. As soon as Billy did that, the whistle blew for half-time, and three of the St Joseph's players fell to the ground, exhausted. They had done nothing but run all game.

'You're doing well,' said Mr Baxter, 'we knew this game was going to be tight.'

'Doing well?' said Gavin quietly. 'I don't think I've touched the ball more than five times.'

'We can't keep this up for the rest of the second half,' said Eugene. He pointed to his teammates, who were still stretched out on the floor. 'Look how tired they are.'

'You three,' said Mr Baxter, looking at the boys who were lying down, 'make sure you get plenty of water. You'll be fine. And you,' he said, turning to Jerome, 'we are going to give you twenty-five minutes. Make them count.'

'Yes, sir,' said Jerome.

'So listen everyone,' said Mr Baxter. 'We just need to keep them from scoring until the last half hour. Then we can start to attack. Keep it tight till then, and we will be OK. Just stick to the tactics.'

The referee blew his whistle to start the second half, and inside four minutes Mr Baxter's tactics were destroyed. In that time, Kingsview scored twice. The first goal came when one of their players tackled Gavin Bradley at kick-off, passed it wide to the left winger, then ran into the area to score a header from the winger's cross. As Mr Baxter called for his players to relax, telling them that it was only one goal and nothing to worry about, Kingsview scored again. The ball came out from a corner to one of their midfielders, and he drove it through a crowd of players. Billy didn't see it until it was too late.

After the second goal, Mr Baxter went straight over to Jerome. 'You have to get in there now,' he said. He waved over to take someone off the pitch and, because of the sun, Jerome didn't see who it was at first. *Oh wow*, thought Jerome, as he saw the teammate trudging towards him. It was Gavin Bradley.

'It's just not happening for you today, Gavin,' said Mr Baxter. 'Jerome, you are playing up top.'

Gavin was so angry that he tried to shove past Jerome, but Jerome stopped him, put his hands on his shoulders and looked him in the eyes. 'See you in the final,' he said. 'Kingsview are going out.'

'Jay-Jay,' came a chant from the heart of the crowd. 'Jay-Jay. Jay-Jay!' As Jerome walked on to the pitch, he clapped his hands high above his head, as if he were singing to the crowd at a rock concert. The crowd clapped back.

'Pretty cocky for a guy who's been on the bench,' said one of their players. 'Thought you were their wonder-boy.'

'You have a plan for me,' said Jerome. 'But we have a plan for you.' He walked over to his teammates. 'Every single time you give me the ball,' he said, 'hit it to me as hard as you can.'

'You sure?' asked Toby.

'Trust me,' said Jerome.

The first three times his team gave Jerome the ball, Jerome didn't touch it. The ball flew past him and on to the Kingsview goalkeeper. 'These lot can't pass,' said one of their defenders. 'This lad is quick, but he is never getting to that. Let's step up.' The defence walked five yards forward, towards the halfway line, near where Jerome was standing. The next time St Joseph's got the ball, they smashed it to Jerome again. The defenders relaxed. What a terrible pass – it was too hard, too high! There was no way Jerome was going to get to that!

But then, too late, they saw Jerome jump. They saw him fling his left foot into the air, so high, almost as high as the crossbar. Then they saw the ball rest against his foot and then bounce forward, and as soon as it dropped Jerome hit it as hard as he could. As he kicked that ball he screamed, screamed like he wanted to scream when Gavin's granddad kicked him out of the house, screamed like he wanted to scream when he knew he was never going to see his dad again. And the ball flew so fast that the first time most people saw it was when it was rolling back out of the net.

'Come on!' screamed Jerome. He thrust his hand in the air, opening and closing it three times: *five, five, five.* 'Come on!' He looked to the side of the pitch where Ian and his family were leaping in the air and so many students were hugging each other. His teammates came to celebrate with him; he waved them away. 'That's nothing,' he said. 'We are still losing. Let's do this!'

For the next twenty-five minutes, two Kingsview players followed Jerome everywhere. Any time the ball came near him, someone pushed or kicked him. But Jerome didn't care. He just got up and jogged away with a smile on his face. St Joseph's gradually became more confident, and it was Kingsview who started to look tired. They tried everything but Billy kept making save after save and they just couldn't score. With ten minutes to go, St Joseph's got a corner. Jerome went over to take it and swung the ball in towards the near post. The referee blew his whistle. One of the Kingsview midfielders had tried to stop it with his arm. *Penalty!*

As Jerome went over to take it, one of the defenders came over to him. 'We know where you are going to put it,' he whispered.

No, you don't, thought Jerome. He put the ball on the spot and walked backwards, remembering what Ian had told him: '*If you can keep your head up when you kick it, then you can see which way goalkeeper is going to jump. That way, you can see all of his clues.'*

Jerome ran towards the ball, watching the goalkeeper all the time. The goalkeeper looked so nervous. He dived all the way to his left. With his left foot, Jerome drove the ball into the other corner of the net. 2–2!

Jerome grabbed the ball from the net, then ran back to the halfway line, placing it on the centre circle. 'The job's not done,' he cried. 'It's not done!' His teammates didn't celebrate this time. Now they were just as ready to win as he was. And they needed to be ready. For the next nine minutes, Kingsview attacked, attacked, attacked. St Joseph's could not get out of their own half. With less than a minute to go, Kingsview got a corner. Even Jerome went back towards his own goal to defend, standing on the edge of his area.

The ball came in from the corner, high, swerving and fast: and Jerome knew what was coming, so he started to run. Billy leapt above the crowd of players, put his fists together, shouted 'Jerome!' and punched the ball straight ahead of him. The ball soared through the air, up and out of the penalty area, and everyone in the crowd turned to watch it fall. And that's when they saw Jerome near the centre circle, rushing at full speed. No one was quick enough to catch him. As the ball landed, Jerome jumped forward to meet it, catching it on the laces of his left boot. He sprinted over the halfway line, knocking the ball forward. It was just him and the goalkeeper now.

His heart was leaping about inside his chest.

And then Jerome remembered Ian's voice: '*When you are running towards goal, all by yourself, I want you to think of this music. Imagine that Erik Satie is playing piano in your head...*'

And suddenly even though the crowd was going wild and everyone around him was shouting, all Jerome could hear in his head was piano music. And he calmed right down. His heartbeat turned slow and soft, like a gentle tap on the window. He came to the edge of the area and he looked the goalkeeper in the eyes, and he saw that the goalkeeper was afraid again. And the goalkeeper came towards him and Jerome quickly leaned to the left, and the goalkeeper fell that same way. Jerome pushed the ball to the right with the outside of his right foot, and it was just him and the open goal. Jerome smashed the ball into the goal, and at once he was screaming again, throwing his hand in the air and doing his celebration, *five, five, five!* He ran towards the crowd. And there was Ian at the corner of the field with his arms out, and Jerome jumped into them.

'You did it, Jerome! You did it!' cried Ian, and they hugged each other. Jerome's teammates arrived and lifted him above their shoulders and into the air. All that Jerome could see was an ocean of happy faces, and he never ever wanted to come down.

24

JUST FINE

As soon as Jerome woke up the next morning, his entire body felt heavy. He was so tired, but as he remembered the day before he was so happy. The moment the match against Kingsview had ended, he felt like a film star. Everyone wanted to talk to him or hug him or shake his hand. 'Thank you, thank you, thank you,' he kept saying. 'Thank you.' By the time he got back to his room someone had already posted the video of all of his goals on social media and thousands of people had watched them. It was like being famous, it really was. Ian asked Jerome's housemaster if he and his family could take Jerome and Stephanie out for dinner, and his housemaster agreed. So they went to Road to Kerala, that lovely curry house in Leytonstone, the same one where Ian was meant to meet Jerome but Jerome didn't turn up.

'So you came here to meet me at last,' said Ian, and everyone laughed. It was one of the best nights of Jerome's life.

The next morning, Jerome sat up in bed and reached for his phone. He had twenty-seven new text messages – messages from Uncle Ray, from Manny, from Reverend Benjamin. 'You superstar!' said one of them. 'Remember us all when you are playing in the Premier League,' said another one. 'So proud to know you,' said another. And then he checked his Instagram, and he gasped. The day before, he had a few hundred followers. Now, he had just over ten thousand. How, how? And then he looked at who was following him. Harvey Masters, the Juventus midfielder! Wesley Mensah, the Ajax right back! Marcello Mandolin, the Real Madrid forward! They must have seen the video of his goals on social media! He looked at his direct messages on Instagram and there were too many to count – hundreds and hundreds!

As he was staring at his phone in amazement, it rang.

'Hey, Mum!' he said.

'Hope you slept well,' she said. 'And don't forget to come home soon. I need you to help with redecorating the flat.'

'OK, Mum,' said Jerome. He didn't really want to go home that day – he wanted to stay in school with his friends and talk about yesterday's match. But he had promised to help his mum, so he had to go back to Hackney.

'I'll need you here at eleven,' she said. 'Don't be late.

I need to do some shopping in the afternoon.'

'No problem at all,' said Jerome. 'I'll be there.'

***

Just over an hour later, Jerome got off the train at Hackney Central and checked his watch. Eleven-fifteen. *Oh no, I'm late!* he thought, and he began to run, past the ticket office and down the hill, out of the station and under the bridge, along the main road, and then left towards his estate. Then as he turned the corner into his estate he heard a huge *boom* as someone pressed play on a very loud piece of music.

'Welcome home, Jerome!' came a voice over the speakers. Jerome looked up towards the first floor of his block of flats and there was Uncle Ray with a microphone, standing behind a set of decks. 'Welcome to the David Emmanuel Estate Soundsystem! Jerome, you are loved, you are blessed! And every tune we play this afternoon is for you!'

As Jerome looked all along the first floor, he saw so many of his friends there, smiling down at him and waving. There was everyone from church. There was Steve, his coach at Hackney Stallions. And so many of the players – Victor, Liam, Lucas, Rob, Jason, Ade. Toby from school was there! And there was Michelle, that lovely girl who always made him feel funny when he looked at her. As he looked at her now, he felt funny again. And ... wow, wait! There were the people who drove him back from Brighton – Roland and Marie. There was Mrs Malone. *Oh no,* thought Jerome, *I need to say sorry to her, I was not very polite to her when I saw her last time.* But she looked so happy to see him. *It will be OK,* he told himself. *I know I make mistakes sometimes, but I'll be just fine.* Then he thought of someone who had made a big mistake. *Aaron,* he thought, *I wish you were here too.*

Jerome heard feet running towards him, and he turned to his left. He heard two voices yelling his name:

'Jerome!'

'Jerome!'

It was Tobi and Femi, Mrs Ayandele's twins. He opened his arms and caught one of them in each.

'Jerome, we saw your goals on the video!' said Tobi. 'The best one was the one when you ran all the way!'

'No!' said Femi. 'The best one was when he kicked it from very far! He just went bang with his foot! And the goalkeeper could not even stop it!'

'Calm down, you two,' laughed Mrs Ayandele, running after them. 'You can like which goals you like!'

'Which one of us is right?' asked Tobi.

'Yes, tell us!' said Femi.

'You are both right,' said Jerome, laughing. 'You are the best twins in the world.'

'God bless you, Jerome,' said Mrs Ayandele. 'You have done so well.'

Jerome's mum came down the steps, wearing a bigger smile than anyone.

'Mum,' said Jerome. 'This is amazing. Thank you so much.'

'I thought it would be a nice surprise,' she said. 'We didn't have much time to plan. But everyone wanted to come and celebrate you. We are so proud of you.' She put an arm around his shoulders. 'Your father is watching you, and he is proud of you too.'

'Oh, Mum,' said Jerome.

'And look,' said Stephanie. 'We have someone to help us decorate.'

Ian walked down the steps to greet them, wearing a white baseball cap and large white workman's overalls, and carrying two paintbrushes in his hands. He handed one of them to Jerome.

'No rest for you, young man,' he said with a grin. 'I've already got started on the living room. You'd better get changed and catch up!'

'Sure thing,' said Jerome, laughing.

'And while we are painting,' said Ian, 'we can talk about all the clubs who were watching you against Kingsview, because they all called the school this morning, very impressed. Everyone was there, and they all want you to go on trial.'

'Wait, who is everyone?' asked Jerome.

'Arsenal, Liverpool, Manchester United. Juventus. Borussia Dortmund. Real Madrid.' As Ian said each name, Jerome's eyes grew wider. 'And if you like,' said Ian, 'I'm happy to drive you to the trials.'

'Oh, Ian,' said Stephanie. 'You are so kind.'

'It is my pleasure, Stephanie,' said Ian. 'You have a special young man, and I'll always help him however I can.'

Jerome could not believe how good this day was. Everything was so perfect. But there was something he still had to say.

'Mum, Ian,' he said. 'I never told you the real reason why I ran away. It was because Gavin was really nasty to me when I went to his house in the country.' Jerome explained what had happened in the hot tub, and how Gavin's granddad had made him leave.

'That's terrible,' said Ian. 'But to be honest, I'm not surprised, and I'm going to have a word with the school about this. I just wish you had told me, Jerome. You will tell me next time, won't you?'

'I promise,' said Jerome.

'Good man. Now, let's paint, let's listen to some good records, and then let's eat. How does that sound?'

'It sounds,' said Stephanie, 'like a very good plan.'

'Excellent,' said Ian, and he walked back towards the staircase.

Jerome looked up at his estate and at all the faces full of joy as the music floated down towards his ears. 'You are my beautiful people,' a woman sang. 'You are my beautiful people.' The sun peered over the edge of the building and a few of its rays rested gently on his shoulders. Jerome stretched out his arms towards the sky, as if he was trying to catch its warmth, and he closed his eyes. For the first time in many years, he knew that this was his home.

ABOUT THE AUTHORS

IAN WRIGHT is one of the UK's all-time leading goal scorers. A Golden Boot winner, he's lifted the Premier League title, The FA Cup and the European Cup Winners' Cup.

MUSA OKWONGA is an author, poet, journalist and musician; he is a co-host of the Stadio football podcast.